THE SWORD'S END

BOOK ONE

<u>COMING SOON</u>

The Sword's End: Book Two

Deicide* (with Kevin Duffield)

(* - working title)

THE SWORD'S END

BOOK ONE

by

Lowell Ellington

Cover Art by Steve Clarke

Cover design by Steve Clarke and Lowell Ellington

For more of Steve Clarke's artwork, check out his galleries at:
http://smg.photobucket.com/albums/v639/escelce/

First Edition: December 2007

ISBN 978-0-6151-7612-3

Published by Lowell Ellington

Printed in the United States of America

To Jacen and Shelly

I love you both!

ACKNOWLEDGMENTS

For my wife, thanks for putting up with my endless ranting and furnishing me with some needed criticism. For my parents and little sister, thanks for the support and praise you've bestowed upon me. For my son, thanks for giving my life purpose. For Connie, thanks for your support throughout the years. For Steve Clarke, who brought my vision to life with his magnificent cover art. For my Grandma Fravel, who supplied my long-distance support. For my friends and their families, thanks for the drive and encouragements I needed to continue on. Finally, I wish to give a special thanks to my editors, Stephanie and Rhonda, for making my late night writing binges legible.

A WORD FROM THE AUTHOR

Usually an author likes to leave his/her notes at the end of the story, but I wanted to beat you to the punch.

I'd like to start off by thanking you for picking up this book (purchased or borrowed, it doesn't matter). It's the story that should matter and I hope you enjoy reading it as much as I did writing it.

What you hold now in your hands, or have downloaded into your computer, is a ten+ years labor of love. I began the story with a blank sheet of paper and one line that kept nagging the back of my mind: "Bastion's wounds have reopened." From there, a whole new world exploded for me. The people and places became a real part of me and haunted me for their completion during my slow periods.

Being a self-published piece, you are bound to find the occasional typos and grammatical mistakes. Those are mine and mine alone. Ironically, English was not my strongest subject in school. I have tried, to the best of my ability, to track down and correct as many as I could find. I know there are some still hidden throughout the book, but please don't let them distract you from the story.

I'll leave you alone now. I've said my piece and the rest is up to you. So, take care and enjoy.

Thanks, again,

Lowell Ellington

BOOK ONE

CHAPTER ONE

"Bastion's wounds have reopened."

This is not what Nix wanted to hear. Cursing the group's misfortunes, he stopped. "How bad is it? Can you control the bleeding until we find shelter?"

"The wound runs deep. It's a miracle he's even survived such a blow."

"Shut up and answer the damn question! Yes or no?!" Nix normally maintained a strong sense of control; unfortunately now was not one of those times.

"Yes," Gavin informed his impatient leader. He knew Nix was worried about their friend. Hell, they all were. But, taxed of any potions to vanquish his dying friend's wounds, he had to rely entirely on his limited experience in first aid. "We'll have to stop for a . . ."

"Do it," Nix ordered. He didn't have time to waste on the wizard's senseless ranting, not when Bastion's life hung in the balance.

"The rain will be coming soon," Twyla felt compelled to inform whoever cared to listen.

"Are you sure?" Nix inquired to prove he was indeed listening. "The sky looks clear to me."

"The trees don't lie," Twyla simply answered.

"How soon?"

A moment of silence passed as Twyla seemed to have

withdrawn into herself. Nix knew of her link to the woods and forced himself to wait for her answer.

"Soon," the elven woman finally revealed. "Strong winds carrying destruction from the east." To enforce her statement, a circle of nearby leaves began a spiraling dance skyward. "Not much time left."

"Great." Massaging away an inevitable migraine, Nix took in his surroundings. The trees would provide some protection, but not enough. Not with Bastion. They needed more. From the way Twyla sounded, they wouldn't even have the time to build a proper shelter. They needed to find something, and soon. "Twyla, scout ahead. See if you can find anything we can use for a shelter. Maybe a cave or something. Make sure we can get Bastion there safely – and no mountain ranges this time."

"You'll never forgive me for that, will you?" Her face told Nix that his words had struck harder than intended.

He gave a simple smile to tell Twyla that all was right. Patting the elf on her rear, Nix sent her on her way. "Go, before it starts raining."

Watching the slender woman sprint off into the forest, Nix lost himself, for a second, in thoughts of her. The way her short-cropped auburn hair came alive as she made her descent electrified his blood. The way her leggings clung to her . . . the restrained breasts in her . . . but, her lips. Her . . .

"Nix!"

"Huh?" He tried to focus.

"Nix. I need your help." Gavin finally succeeded in gaining his attention.

Ashamed of having been caught off guard, Nix rushed to

his friend's aid. "What's wrong? Is he in shock? Are . . . ?"

"Shut up for a minute." It was Gavin's turn to silence Nix. "I need you to talk to Bastion while I tend to his wounds. We must keep him awake."

Letting the amateur wizard address the wound, for the third time, he had no idea where to begin the conversation. "That was some fight, huh?" Glancing down toward Bastion's bloodied chest, after Gavin removed the soaked rags from it, he bit his tongue for his choice of opening conversation topics.

"Fight?" a weakened Bastion managed to force out.

"You should have seen yourself. I couldn't be prouder. You fought like a true warrior."

"Bu . . . llshit. You're the warr . . . ior."

"Give yourself some credit. You put up a good fight."

An air of silence worried Nix, prompting him to slap the wounded thief across the face. "Hey! Stay awake."

"I said talk to him, not beat him senseless," Gavin intervened.

"I'm trying, damn it!" He knew Gavin didn't deserve the outburst. He only hoped his friend knew it, too.

"I . . . 'm cold," Bastion whispered into the wind.

Relief poured through the warrior's body and he instantly relinquished his worn-out cloak. It did nothing to warm the man, but it did give Nix's soul some comfort to aid his injured friend. "There you go. Worry not, buddy, Twyla will be back soon. Then we'll get you to safety."

A brief pause in his work allowed Gavin to look up at Nix's progress. Alarms sounded off in his head as he saw Nix prepare to quench the thief's thirst with the water supplied in his wineskin. "No!" he cried out once he had possession of the container. "No water. In his weakened condition, he could drown himself on even the shallowest of swallows." The tone in his voice told Nix not to chance it.

"I have to do something to ease his pain."

"All right. All right already! I'll talk to him. Since you want something to do so badly, why don't you build something we can transport him on."

"Which is something we should have done in the first place," Nix reprimanded himself.

"Hey, that's why you're the leader. So stop with the self-pity crap and get started. Twyla should be back . . . well, speaking of the elven wench," Gavin popped off.

Twyla's snarled lips and icy glare were all the wizard needed to remind him not to try her patience. "Shelter is not far. I found a small clearing. Looks like there's a shrine of some sort, resting in its center. But, safe enough for our needs."

Nix marveled at the elf's stamina, she was not even breaking a sweat. "How far away?"

"Not far. Just past the grove of sassafras. If we leave now, we can get there before it rains."

"Where?" Nix was confused.

Pointing in an eastern direction, Twyla shook off her mild annoyance toward his human ignorance. "Over the hill."

"Great," Nix felt back in control of the situation. "Gavin. Can we carry Bastion there?"

"Not a chance."

"Twyla. Do we have time to build a stretcher?"

"No."

"Think, Nix. Think." Returning his fingertips to massaging his temples, he tried to ignite the fuel in his brain and come up with the answer that they were denied. "Carrying him is out. No time for a stretcher . . . "

"Nix?" Gavin tried to get his leader's attention.

"Give me a moment," Nix could barely speak as he paced around in circles and stopped. A glance up at the wizard told him that the two of them were thinking on the same path. It was the only way.

Twyla stepped back.

"Are you sure you can do it?" Nix felt compelled to ask.

"Do I really have a choice?"

He told him straight out, "No."

Twyla moved back even further.

Resigning to the fact that it was do or die, given Bastion's situation, Gavin opted to avoid the latter. A brief scan into the well-cared-for book that held his spells, and he refreshed his memory. Coughing abruptly to clear his throat, he began the incantation.

Nix remembered Gavin's earlier attempts at spell casting and followed Twyla's lead by distancing himself, as well.

Five minutes later, sweat decorated the wizard's brow and the 'danger' was over. No one was as surprised as Gavin to observe Bastion rise and float comfortably on a cushion of air. "I did it! Twyla! Nix! I did it!", he exclaimed.

"Hold the celebration," Nix flatly declared. "We have to hurry. The clouds are already blackening."

The wind was in high gear by the time they reached the clearing, but the spell still safely suspended the fallen comrade. Due to the unpredictable length of the spell, they carefully hurried toward the building ahead of them. Walking as if being pallbearers, they moved aside of Bastion as he was carried along on the magickal cushion of air. Each was preparing themselves to catch the wounded thief, if and when the spell should wear off.

Having finally made their way into the destined opening, the group shared Twyla's earlier assessment about how much the building resembled a shrine. It stood alone in the small clearing. Vines and miscellaneous vegetation clung to the building's marble exterior. No markings or symbols of any race or religion adorned it. The building only stood a mere fifteen feet tall with a base of twenty feet. *Not much to look at. Hope there's enough room inside for all of us. But at least we'll be out of the storm's way,* Nix fathomed.

The entrance, they noticed, was once protected by a sturdy iron gate. But, thanks to weather conditions and improper maintenance, the gate now hung limply by one rusted hinge. Swinging to and fro, aided by the winds from the upcoming storm, an eerie creak was produced that managed to provide a chill that ran down each group member's back.

"I don't like this." Gavin was the first to speak up, causing them to stop and reconsider their decision about entering.

"We have no say in the matter." Allowing himself one

large gulp of air to subside his nerves, Nix went in.

"This doesn't feel right," Twyla confided.

"You're the one that picked the spot. Remember? Now you're having second thoughts?" Gavin couldn't help but modify her own restlessness into his own. "Ask the trees. They might have some answers for you," he mocked.

"They do not answer." This didn't help matters. "I can't even sense them here. I never entered the clearing when I found it. I just saw the building and came back for you guys. Maybe I should have, at least, looked *in* the building?"

"It's safe," Nix interrupted his companions' flow of conversation as he stuck his head out of the doorway. "Get Bastion in here."

Obeying the order, they entered and reality screeched to a halt. The room they expected to see was not as they imagined. The exterior had betrayed the interior. While, on the outside, the building was relativity small, the inside showed more room than was physically possible. The room was also lavishly decorated with expensive tapestries, statues cast from silver and gold, and enough treasure to make the oldest of dragons jealous because of their impotent hordes. The dream of every wandering adventurer was right here in their grasp.

Atop the treasure, high above, rested a throne. A throne that knew no equal. Carved from ivory, two faces made up the armrests, one male and one female. The sides were encrusted with gems and stones of various colors and clarity. From where the group stood, far below, the stones appeared to merge together, forming the illusion of a face on either side. The stone faces were the same as the ivory faces on the armrests. The female stone face appeared on the side with the male ivory face, and vice versa . . . The back of the throne, however, was blocked. Its owner still resided there. The skeletal remains of a long dead human could be seen from the floor.

"This place is huge," Twyla marveled. "Magick lives within these walls."

"True. I can feel it's warm presence flowing through me as we speak," Gavin agreed. "A powerful magick, at that. Given the amount of wealth that adorns these walls, I'd say that we are the first visitors this place has had in years."

"Truly a thief's paradise . . . BASTION!"

The memory of their dying friend caused the two of them to quickly turn their attention on him. As Gavin released the spell's hold, Twyla made herself useful by searching the room for anything usable for a fire. A wooden chair of exquisite beauty was quickly decimated and placed into use. Before long, the elven woman had a roaring fire going that supplied Bastion with the warmth he needed. By this time, Gavin had replaced the bloodied wrappings around the chest wound with fresh ones.

Oblivious to the world around him, Nix was drawn to the skeletal figure. He heard his friends, in the back of his mind, but couldn't comprehend what it was they were saying. The only thing that dominated his mind was the skeleton. He had to see it. He *needed* to see it.

The skeleton bore no remains of flesh, but Nix instantly knew that it was once a man. Not out of instinct, but because of the armor that still gave it support. The emblem that adorned the breastplate, two lions entwined at the hip with a dragon towering over the two, was unfamiliar and unimportant. What truly captivated his soul was the former warrior's choice of weapon.

Nestled in the warrior's bony grasp was a sword of great beauty. No dust or webbing laid claim to its surface. Streams of light cascaded off its four feet of polished metal. Using the streams of light as evidence, Nix concluded that Twyla must have the fire going by now. *Good*, he thought. *Bastion is in good hands.*

Minute explosions of dust and bone fragments erupted from the dead warrior's left hand as Nix broke off each of its stiff fingers that held onto the sword's hilt. He had to see the complete work of art its maker had forged.

The hilt, itself, was at least a foot long. Unsure as to whether it was simply lined or cast solid, the handle looked to be forged in gold. Fashioned into the shape of a young, voluptuous woman clothed in a long, form-fitting gown, it showed a look of tranquility. A smooth, crystal surface encased the woman and helped to hold in the soft clouds of smoke wrapping around the figure, thus completing the hilt.

After prying the sword's tip out of the warrior's left foot, he was fascinated at the exceptional balance it maintained in his grasp. "Truly a weapon for a warrior," Nix voiced to no one in particular. Finding the sword's scabbard next to the throne, he attached it to his belt and slid the sword into place. Claiming it as his own, he walked down the flight of stairs that led to the throne and rejoined his friends.

"Finished?" Twyla popped off, not allowing Nix even a glance.

"Yeah."

"Good." A sense of uneasiness could be felt flowing off of her. "Our food is scarce. I'm going out to bring some back."

"In the storm?" Gavin's attention was on her now.

"We need food," was her only excuse.

"Be careful out there." The tone of Nix's voice informed her that he understood her unspoken comment.

Twyla's smile was his reward as she left.

*　　*　　*

Where Twyla managed to locate two rabbits in the strong winds of the storm was beyond her companions' minds. But the scent of roasted meat had filled the room, reminding the entire party just how hungry they really were. It also helped Bastion get his mind off his pain.

After eating, Nix tossed an armload of another broken chair into the blazing fire. "It's been a long day. I'll take first watch," he declared. Of course, Gavin declined to protest. Twyla, on the other hand, was a little reluctant and accepted with the stimulation of having the second watch.

Curling up in front of the fire, the elf and wizard soon departed the conscious world and permitted themselves to be lifted away to the land of dreams. That was, after they had checked on Bastion's condition. He would live to fight another battle and steal another man's purse, they assured themselves.

Time passed while the companions slept and Nix occupied himself with his new sword. Clutching the hilt in his right hand, he twisted the blade around to allow the fire's light to show off

24

its exquisite craftsmanship. The sword's weight gave no hint as to its presence. Its weight was like that of a shaft arrow from Twyla's quiver, next to nothing. Although the hilt gave the impression of having a smooth, slick surface, the sword was in no danger of leaving his grasp. Somehow, the warmth from his hand changed the hilt's contour. The crystal layer around the golden woman actually reconstructed itself to allow Nix a comfortable and flexible hold. Also, he was thrilled to find out, its balance equaled its beauty: flawless. He couldn't tear himself away from his sense of wonderment. It was like he had just been reunited with a lost part of his soul he never knew was missing. The sword became a part of him.

A thought of concern pried his mind away from the sword and caused him to focus, for a second, on his sleeping friends. Twyla finally stopped tossing around from discomfort and found peace in herself, allowing sleep to claim her. Unlike Gavin, who had no such restraints holding him back. The fire still had some life left to it and Bastion was still unconscious. Everything was in order.

2

The silken gown flowed around my bare legs as the tight corset hugged my waist and bosom. Hours of self-preparation went into this moment and I could barely contain myself to allow the next few to arrive. A final check in the wall-embedded mirror showed me that my hair was still as flawless as it was the last time I felt the urge to check on its condition, a mere few minutes beforehand. Allena, my lady-in-waiting, fills me with constant reassurances that the herbs and powders are applied properly to my face. I had to be perfect and Allena knew of my nervousness all to well.

"Your beauty could not be more heavenly, M'lady. My skills would only flaw your perfection, at this point. I can do no more," she admitted to me. I could feel the pride she projected in the fine work she accomplished. Or was it my nervousness I was sensing? I couldn't tell.

"I've waited for this day to come my whole life," I confided. "But, now that it has arrived, I find that I'm forcing myself to carry on."

"You question your love for him?" Allena was forced to ask.

"Of course, I love him! I love Lucian more as each new day blossoms into view. It's just that I wonder about my own capabilities of serving him properly as his wife. I fear that I shall not be able to fulfill my duties to him."

For all the years she has served me, I knew that Allena had prepared herself for my lack of self-confidence. She knew me, like I said before, all too well. "That's nonsense. Any man would sever any appendage to claim you as his wife."

My eyebrows showed her that her choice of words was questionable. "Alright, maybe not any appendage," she corrected herself with a sudden burst of laughter.

I joined in. It made me feel better. I realized, at that moment, I was just being silly. I was stupid for believing we were anything but perfect for each other. We had a ten-year *engagement span to prove it. Weddings, simply, just had a way of bringing out the worst fears in a person. I knew, however, that I would persevere.*

A strong, firm hug enforced our friendship even further. She was my best friend. I would be lost without her. "Thanks for being here, Allena."

"It's my pleasure, M'lady."

"Sasha," I interrupted. "Please, call me Sasha, my friend."

I don't believe she was prepared for that. Her facial expression said as much. But, the smile that widened on her face also told me it touched her inside."Yes, . . . Sasha."

We hugged, again.

"Enough of this mushy stuff," I resigned myself to admit. "I have a wedding to go to."

*   *   *

"Nix?" Twyla called out.

"Huh? Allena?" Nix mumbled as he tried to regain familiarity in his surroundings. Sleep has a way of robbing people of their senses.

"Allena?" Twyla asked. A brisk slap across the face snapped her delirious leader awake. "Wake up! Damn it!"

"I'm awake! I'm awake, already!" Nix screamed at his assailant. "A simple nudge would have sufficed."

"Bastion is dead."

"WHAT?!"

"While you were *maintaining* your watch, someone came in and slit his throat!" she informed him. Her face was a mixture of fear and disgust. *How could you let this happen,* her eyes demanded from Nix.

27

A mad dash over to Bastion's cold, dead body confirmed Twyla's words. Rigor mortis froze the young man's face into a mummified mask of terror that ripped away a portion of Nix's soul. The gash on the throat gave evidence as to how he died, but the body being bone dry, due to being completely drained of blood, added the flavor of mystery. "My god, what have I done? How could I have let this happen?" Clutching the body in his arms, Nix released a fury of emotions that betrayed his warrior's training. Tears flowed freely from his eyes as he cried his grief and damned his own soul. "I have failed you," he whispered to the lifeless corpse. "I have failed you."

Having been awakened by the outbursts of screams and curses, Gavin stood silently beside Twyla and watched as Nix exploded in an uncontrollable rage directed to the surrounding artifacts. Tapestries were torn from the walls, while piles of golden treasure and coins took to the air as Nix delivered a series of hate-driven kicks. "I vow on my very soul that I shall find and kill the bastard who robbed you of your life!" he swore to the heavens. Drawing out his sword, he slide the blade across his left palm and sealed his words in blood. The act of the blood oath made Gavin stop and reconsider his decision to try and calm his friend down. Silence suited him fine, just now.

Twyla, on the other hand, maintained a focused mind. Taking in all the information she could gather, she walked over to her former friend's body. The lack of blood was what worried her the most. There should be, at least, some soaked into the ground. There was none. The body's coldness suggested that he had been murdered shortly after they fell asleep last night. Possibly an hour or a half after she, herself, fell asleep. *But*, she wondered, *if someone was to come in here and murder Bastion, why weren't the rest of us slaughtered? Why only him? It doesn't make sense.*

Unfortunately for them, sense was something that would not grasp them for a while to come.

*   *   *

High above, watching over the group's actions, the skeletal warrior's lifeless body sat. For over a century, it had laid claim to its ivory throne. Its eternal grin appeared to mock the mourners below. A tiny bead of blood made its way down a bony hand and dripped off one of the broken fingers that once clenched the sword.

3

It was the next day before they were able to build Bastion's funeral pyre. The blazing summer sun had evaporated all signs of yesterday's storm and left the surrounding clearing of land acceptable for the ceremony. The spot Twyla chose for the pyre to be built was far enough away from the trees to please her. The last thing she wanted was to have her friend's funeral cause a flaming wave of death and destruction to spread throughout her beloved forest.

Once the spot had been chosen, Gavin prepared the body for its final voyage. Nix and Twyla, meanwhile gathered the necessary wood.

Silence accompanied the two friends as they entered the forest's domain to begin their search. Nix veered off to the right and hoped that his female companion would choose another path to follow. She didn't.

Now is not the time to leave him alone, she decided. Knowing that her company was unwelcome did not dissuade her from following him in any way. She didn't care what he wanted, because whether he wanted one or not, she felt she had to remind him that there was still a friend he could turn to, if needed.

Nix was aware of Twyla's intentions and appreciated her concern, but there were times when a person needed to be left alone. Now was one of those times. Grinding the dead leaves under his boots into twisted balls, he sharply swung around and thrust his index finger out. He barely missed pegging the elf's nose. "Whatever form of a leash you have attached to me, sever it now!" he growled at her. "I don't want your company. I don't need companionship, a traveling buddy, or a blasted shoulder to cry on." Grinding his teeth together, he made it a point to emphasize his last choice of words, "JUST . . . LEAVE . . . ME . . . **ALONE**!"

"No," the elven maiden stated evenly. "I will not."

The veins protruded on his temples, as his temper rose, giving a clear indication as to the seriousness of the warrior's words. His angered eyes begged with Twyla to allow him his solitude. The elf stood her ground. Whether he needed her or not, she was determined to be there for him now. Even if it killed her.

"It's not your fault." Tired of waiting on him to make the first move, she jumped into the direct approach. "It could happe . . ."

"Happen to anyone? Happen to anyone! No, it couldn't! It happened to me. It was my watch. My responsibility. Don't you see? If I would have stayed awake, Bastion would still be alive right now. But I fell asleep!" Tears of rage made their way out of his eyes, at that point. "I am the one that deserves that pyre, not Bastion."

About time we get somewhere, Twyla thought. "How can you stand there and tell me that load of crap? I can place the blame just as easily on myself. We all fell asleep. You're only human, after all." *Uh-oh*, Twyla thought, as she realized her poor choice of words.

"Don't you *dare* bring my race into this, *elf*!"

"It wasn't meant as an insult, my friend. It's just a common phrase I've heard your people say several times." Twyla made a mental note to give herself a swift kick in the rear, for that blunder. "Now stop trying to change the subject."

Helpless against her verbal assault, Nix plopped himself down in front of a giant oak. "He was my friend," he mumbled toward the ground.

"And mine as well," she reminded him.

"But I was his leader. He looked to me for guidance and the only thing I led him to was his death."

"It was his choice to follow you. You hung nothing over his head that forced him along. It was his decision, not yours."

"But, I . . . " Nix tried to butt in.

"But, nothing." Crouching down to his level, she placed her left hand on his shoulder. "Not long ago, I remember a similar conversation being told to a young, naive, elven girl. Memory recalls that she also blamed herself for another one's death. A very dear friend was lost to her, due to her poor judgment."

Nix raised his head as he, too, remembered the very same tale. The tears in his eyes almost obstructed his view of Twyla's warming smile. Funny how time has a way of repeating itself.

31

"Derek's death hurt me as much as Bastion's does you," she stated. "And they are not going to be the only friends that are going to be lost to us. Life has a way of robbing us of our loved ones. But it also grants us the privilege of encountering new ones," she explained. "So, as you sit there mourning our lost friend and damning yourself for it, remember there are still others here who count you among their friends. May peace find you." Softly moving the hair from his forehead, she planted a loving kiss upon it as she ended her words.

Feeling that she could do no more for him, she granted her leader his solitude and hoped her words got through to him. She had to get back to gathering wood for the pyre.

Startled by a hand on her shoulder, she turned back toward Nix, who now stood up before her.

"I . . ." he shamefully whispered. "I need a shoulder."

Twyla was more than happy to accommodate him.

*   *   *

Nix touched the flaming torch to the wooden pyre's base and watched as the dry twigs accepted the flame. As the fire spread, he stepped back and rejoined his friends. The body that rested on top was cloaked entirely in the wrappings that Gavin provided. The ceremony called for it. It is believed that the soul of the person must be contained until the gods granted them access into their domain. The cloak prevented the soul from being scattered by the smoke that crept around it. The ceremony must also be done in silence. So there the three friends stood, and paid their reverence until the fire's might diminished.

32

4

No one wanted to sleep that night, even though their bodies craved it. Bastion's murder was enough to keep them conscious. Unwilling to step back into the shrine's enchanted walls, Twyla's uneasiness about the building prompted her to suggest that they camp inside the forest's protective realm. Nix agreed. Gavin followed. Of the three of them, none had any objections to leaving.

An hour of travel provided them a safe distance and showed them a small area where they decided to set up camp. Respecting the other two's temporary dislike of fire, Gavin volunteered to build it. Twyla occupied herself with clearing away the dead leaves and twigs that covered the ground. While the others were busy, Nix began to rummage through his backpack with the intent of rationing out the dried meat stored in it.

After everything was done and the fire had enough fuel to supply itself throughout the night, they ate. The dry, salted meat was hardly the nourishment their stomachs were calling for, but it would suffice. Eating the meat was like eating leather strips and tasted almost as bad. The weak wine Gavin carried in his wineskin helped to kill the taste, though.

"Where are we headed for now, chief?" Gavin asked in hopes that it would spark a conversation. The silence was wearing him a bit thin.

"We keep the same direction we were heading in," Nix answered. "To the town of Jenna."

"Jenna?" Twyla could hardly believe it. "That's clear on the other side of the plains!"

Nix expected the reaction, True, Jenna was at least three

33

seasons worth of travel, by foot. For some odd reason, unbeknownst to him, he felt drawn there. Reading the faces of his friends, he knew he was asking a lot, especially from Twyla. It would mean for her to distance herself from the beloved forest she called home. Nix was gambling on the friendship she had spoken of earlier to prod her along.

Twyla's mind was in a frenzy. *What's in Jenna that would make him want to trek that far? Is it to gain distance from here? Did Bastion's death affect him more than I fathomed?* Well, she concluded, *he wouldn't go unless it was important, At least, for his sake, it better be.* "We're going to need horses."

"No shit!", Gavin exclaimed after he got over his initial shock.

Rubbing the blood-soaked cloth that bound the gash on his left palm, Nix prayed that by the time they reached their destination he would know why he had taken them there.

CHAPTER TWO

To the average observer, the mountain ranges in the northern part of the mainland looked forbidding and impassable. However, those with enough courage and determination might find the small trail that was entangled within a crevice of rock and snow.

The path was only known to a chosen few. Of those few, none would have taken it if they weren't aware of its destination. For hidden in the mountains was the home of the Circle of Elders.

The Circle of Elders, an ancient devotion, was formed back when magick was anew. Though they safeguarded their privacy, they were bound by oath to watch over the world and act as its protectors from the threat of misused magick. Those who practiced the arts, no matter what faction, have heard tales of their presence. But, none harbored any proof as to the Circle's existence. An old master's tale to keep young apprentices in order was the most popular theory to the myth.

Anyway, if one were to take the path to its end, he would view a palace of exquisite beauty. The building itself was no marvel. Its simple structure was fashioned with stone and wood. With a high tower supporting each of the building's four corners and a small water moat surrounding its base, one could not help but call it common. The beauty that made it truly shine, however, was the landscape around it. Trees flourished in a springtime pride. Acres of prosperous woodland stretched for as far as the eye could see. Anyone who paid witness to the site could only bring one word to mind: harmonious. Despite the cold, harsh mountains engulfing the grassy fields, it's basking aura felt natural, particularly to the members of the Circle, who were it's creators.

The inside of the castle was as common as it's exterior. Torches of flame decorated the inner stone hallways. Scattered tapestries and portraits adorned the walls. The ground floor served its use by providing a dining area and a vast library of ancient scrolls and text used to train young pupils. This floor also housed the Circle's conference halls and laboratories that taught herbalism, alchemy, and other such subjects.

As the staircase in the main hall is ascended, the sleeping chambers are revealed. The east wing held the student's chambers, while the west wing gave haven to all but twelve of the teachers, or masters, as they were known by the students. The absent twelve made up the inner circle. They slept elsewhere.

Residing in one of the masters' chambers was Kane. An old man of seventy-eight, he was wise beyond his years. If not for his ailing health, he would surely become one of the rare few bestowed with the title of Elder.

A series of lung-crushing coughs plagued the old master that night. Tossing and turning underneath his frail blankets, his mind was in turmoil while his body suffered. The stuffed sack that served as a pillow was drenched in perspiration.

"Sasha, no!" he called out from his dreams. The words were barely audible and none of his fellow followers heard them from their own rooms. He was alone, at least in the physical form. However, in his mind's eye, he had plenty of company. Visions of people and incidents that took place before his birth swarmed around him. The image of a vigorous man in knight's armor froze before him. The breast plate, which bore two lions and a looming dragon, was familiar. It belonged to Lucian.

"Lucian!" Kane screamed in ghastly horror. His body snapped awake. Scrambling out of bed, his bones cried out their discomfort. Fear blocked his pain as he hurried to put on his crimson robe that rested on a nearby chair. Not caring if he had the garment fully secured or not, he headed from his chamber door. The door remained open as the old man departed the room.

Though the stone tiles that made up the floor of the hallway were cold, he hardly noticed as he scurried down them. Although the torches adorning the walls provided him sight, they were not needed. He knew where he was heading. The familiar passageways were embedded in his memory. He only hoped that his frail body could get him there.

Even with the determination of a man possessed, Kane's aged body failed to supply him with the strength he required. He collapsed a few dozen yards short of his destination: Gessa's room.

"Gessa," he mouthed after his inflamed lungs denied him his voice. *Calm down, you old fool*, he reprimanded himself. *What good will I be if I die before I can warn them?* A moment of self-control was all that was needed for Kane to regain the use of his voice. "Gessa," he tried again. Still weak, it wasn't enough.

Cursing the cruelty of fate's timing, he reached a decision.

Despite the warnings from the Elders, of not tapping into magick in his weakened condition, he had no choice. Casting off a brief string of words from a forbidden spell, Kane extended out his left hand and unleashed a phantasmal force that sped three hundred yards down the corridor of the east wing. Upon impact, it obliterated the wall in its path. Sapped of strength, as he knew he would be, he laughed to himself. *Only the dead could ignore that.* Then the coughing returned with a vengeance.

Doors in the east wing flew open in rapid succession before the first one even opened in the west end. Baffled students bumped into each other while being clouded in the explosion's aftermath.

"Are we being attacked?" one student asked another.

"No one would dare attack the Elders," a young girl corrected her friend once she joined the others in the hallway. Brushing a handful of long, black hair out of her eyes, the girl known as Gessa surveyed her surroundings. To her left were the hollowed remains of a wall that now had a really pleasant view to the outside. Why? What's the point? Walking toward the wall, to get a closer look, a wave of people ran past her. Her head swivelled around to look where everyone was flocking. Her eyes widened as she joined the running crowd and saw the fallen master.

"It's Master Kane."

Kane? Disbelief boggled Gessa's mind. *Who would dare . . . ?*

"Gessa?" a voice called out. "Gessa, he's calling for you."

"Me?" Gessa asked as she approached the fallen figure.

Why would he want me? Kneeling beside her master, she looked into the dying man's eyes. "I'm here, Master."

"Gessa?"

"Yes."

"Gessa," Kane forced out, though the pain in his lungs tried to prevent it. "Y-You . . . mus..t . . . He's re..tur..ned."

"Master, you must not talk. You need to conserve your strength," she tried to counsel her mentor. "Then you can say what needs to be said."

"No!" Kane declared with a sudden burst of force. "He has returned!"

"Who?" the young student asked. "Who has brought forth this sense of urgency in you?"

"Lucian."

"Lucian?" Puzzled, she demanded more information. "Who is Lucian?"

Kane did not answer the question. The magick that was forbidden to him had done its damage. His life force had been depleted. The knowledge of having been able to warn the others comforted him into death's waiting arms. His mission was done.

"Master?" Gessa kept asking her dead mentor's body, to no avail. Tears swelled for the loss of her master and the lost knowledge Kane had yet to teach her. Tears falling unheeded, she stood to face the crowd of confused and saddened students and masters. "Who is Lucian?" she demanded.

*   *   *

Buried deep under the building's foundation was a room

where the Circle of Elders resided. After traveling down a dizzying spiral pattern of narrowly carved stone steps, Gessa came into the Elder's presence.

The room fulfilled her expectations. Little light was permitted down here, allowing the shadows to mingle freely in the background. The single source of light was a torch located in what seemed to be the center of the room. The rays that shone off the torch's dancing flame outlined a seven-foot circular wall surrounding it. Having approached the torch through the small opening that severed part of the wall, she waited.

Determined not to display any lack of discipline, as she was taught, Gessa gave herself no slack and stood straight and proper until she was addressed. A sense of uneasiness caused her to take in the area around her. Alas, no more information was granted to her. She could sense movement, but saw none. Eyes were paying her close attention, she suspected, as the muscles in her legs showed the first signs of cramping up. The fear of them finding any signs of weakness dissuaded her from shifting any weight around.

"Young Gessa," an unseen voice addressed her. "You have been called forth today to begin a journey of unfathomable peril." The echo in the room made it hard for Gessa to decide what direction the voice came from.

Picking up where the first voice left off, a new voice stated, "For close to two hundred years, the world has been safeguarded from the threat of Lucian. The recent . . . demonstration by Master Kane has prompted us to believe that he has, once again, returned to this world."

"But, why me?" Gessa asked before she thought it best not to.

A new voice answered her. "In Kane's final hour, he called out for you, child. With the threat of Lucian being as grave as it is, logic dictates that either we or another one of the masters would have been called for. But, he chose you. That small bit of information has led us to the conclusion that he was secretly training you to continue his mission."

Acting as if they were speaking as one, another voice crept in. "At the time of Lucian's initial defeat, a sword was altered to hold his spirit at bay. To our knowledge, this is the only weapon that can effectively destroy him. If he has returned, the sword must have been removed."

"Excuse me?" Gessa was lost. "You're telling me an evil entity has returned. An altered weapon serves as the only thing that can kill him. The sword was removed and you need me to kill him again. All because Master Kane cried out my name?"

"Yes," the voices said in unison.

"And I'm to take this quest alone, I presume?"

"Yes."

"Do I look stupid?" the young student demanded. *Forget this!* she thought. *Intimidation or not, I don't care who they are. This is suicide!*

The Circle flew into outrage. "How *dare* you speak to us in such a blasphemous tone!" The shock spewed forth in a volley of threats and fits of rage. Silhouettes of the enraged Elders were now found by the torch's light.

"Forgive me," the girl apologized. *I think I just overstepped*

41

my boundaries. "I meant no disrespect. I only meant to object to traveling alone. I've never been outside the mountain's walls before. I don't know how the other world lives, much less how to find my way around it alone.

"I agree the mission is of grave importance. That, I'm not going to argue with you. I gladly accept being chosen, but I need help. At least, one or two of my fellow students."

Shelving their anger, the Elders recognized the logic in the young woman's voice. "Very well, you shall be assigned two other students to aid in your task. Before you leave, we will set up an arrangement in the library for your group to meet. Any more questions?"

"When do I . . . we leave?"

"Tonight."

"Very well, I'll go to prepare." Leaving the bewildered Elders to themselves, Gessa turned and left. But not before she heard one of them comment about how her attitude must have been a contributing factor in Kane's decision.

Gessa smiled.

*   *   *

The library was the meeting place Gessa chose to confront her two candidates to take on the voyage, Thomas and Opal. Not much thought was lost in deciding to ask them first. Thomas, she figured, would be a good pick because of his skills in hunting and wilderness survival. The lad seemed more at home in the wooden acres around them and spent most of his available time studying and camping out there. Opal, on the other hand, would be a valuable asset for her passion of the healing arts and knowledge of ancient languages, elven being her major. The girl spent the majority of her free time deciphering old text books, Gessa often observed. But, if there had to be a key factor that had to tie the two of them together, it was the fact that the two were both sixteen years old. Gessa was their senior by two years, a fact that she intended to use to her advantage.

Gessa noticed the pair sitting at a far off table in the library. They recognized her as she entered. Waving back, she extended an index finger to signal them that she would join them in a second. She had to do something first.

Quickening her pace, Gessa sought out and found the library's Keeper of the Scrolls, Gunthar. Of all the adults she associated with, she felt most at ease around the short, stocky librarian. Gunthar had a way of making the drabbest subjects into a cornucopia of enchantment and wonder. Gessa loved the many hours the two of them shared conversing about anything that came to mind.

"Gessa!" Gunthar called out when he saw the youth. "Over here. I have some books you might be interested in."

"Sorry, I can't now," Gessa respectfully declined. "But, I do need your help."

"Hey, that's what I'm here for." A smile appeared on the short man's face. His heart glowed whenever a student came to him for help. Those times were becoming fewer and fewer as the children grew older. The independence that students craved was the cause of his loneliness amongst the scrolls and text. "Give me a hand and tell me your problem." He then proceeded to pull dusty books off the shelves and place them into Gessa's waiting arms.

She accepted the task and confided in her friend. "I have been chosen for a quest."

"A quest?" The librarian was impressed. Not too many students were gifted with the Circle's attention.

"Yeah. Remember the master who died outside of our chambers?"

"Yes. Kane was a good man. A bit secluded, at times, but a good man, nonetheless. Why? Does it have something to do with him?"

"Partially. Before he died, he called out my name and the Circle thinks that alone qualifies me for the job."

"All this because he called out your name?" Gunthar guessed there was something missing.

"Strange, huh?"

"Interesting would be the word I'd choose."

"It gets more stra . . . interesting. They actually want me to go out and kill somebody, too," Gessa added to her friend's growing confusion. Having followed the girl with his own stack of books, Gunthar listened on. "Apparently, he's a great threat to the world and all that other lame stuff."

"The Circle wants you to kill someone?" Gunthar had to ask to be sure. "The Circle?"

"Yeah. Group of twelve old guys. Big magick. Heard of them?" Gessa laid out with a thick slice of sarcasm.

"Save your attitude for someone else, young lady. Of course, I've heard of them. I might spend most of my time in here, but I'm not ignorant."

"Sorry, I'm just having this feeling that they are not telling me everything."

"Well, what did they tell you?"

"Have you been listening to anything that I've said?"

"It just doesn't sound like something the Circle would do."

"By the way, where did you say you wanted these?" The weight of the books was starting to take their toll on the young girl's arms.

Nudging his head toward a nearby table, Gunthar answered the question. "Over there."

"Anyway, I told you he was this great threat to the world. Personally, I think it's one of those 'prove-yourself-worthy' type of assignments. Nothing serious, just something to test me with. Maybe to see if I could actually kill someone on their order. What do you think?"

"I think . . . " he paused as he set the books down. "I think you might want to take this more seriously. The Circle doesn't send out their pupils on wasteful tasks. They usually leave that to the masters. There might be some truth behind their words which you'd see if you would stop putting this off as a waste of your time."

"Well, *if* it is true, I'll be ready. Trust me."

"I don't need your trust. You do." Gunthar loved it when he could make up little words of wisdom. It made him feel important and wiser.

"Whatever. Anyway, I need to take some books and scrolls

with me. Don't worry. I'll bring them back in one piece."

"Sure, what's the subject you're going to be needing?"

"Anything you got on a man called Lucian." Gessa was glad they had finally reached the real point of the conversation. Opal and Thomas must be growing impatient, by now. She knew that she would be if the situation was reversed.

"Lucian." The name rolled off the librarian's tongue with bitter contempt. "Why, in Sarvon's name, would you seek information about that fiend? He's dead."

"Kane said he has returned," Gessa flatly declared.

Guthar's legs gave out on him, causing the scrawny man to land sharply on his tail bone. "Great gods, preserve us! He's returned?!"

"I guess so." Having extended out the hand to help him up, Gessa needed to satisfy her own curiosity. "Gunthar, who's Lucian? The Circle was rather vague on that point."

"Lucian was . . . is an abomination. He is death to those who approach him," he explained as he walked to the walls which contained the requested information. Sweat seemed to have found its way to the thin man's forehead when he began his explanation. But, instead of dictating the evil one's story, he felt the written words would provide a better description. "Take these. You'll need to read them all and know them by heart. This is no test, girl. This is life and death. Make no mistakes, Lucian is the grave threat that they warned you of. Above all else, though, drop the attitude. It has no place on this quest." All signs of humor had been wiped away from both of their faces.

46

Gessa gulped a breath of air. *Gods, he's serious.* "This is crazy. How can I, an eighteen-year-old girl, fight someone as dangerous as him? I can't do it. They're sending me out there to die!"

"Calm down, child. Use your head. You might not understand why they chose you, but they did. If you go out there thinking that you are going to die, the die you will. You got a strong head on them shoulders of yours and it is about time you took advantage of it."

"I . . . but . . ."

"Stop it! Now!" Gunthar demanded. It was extremely unusual for him to command such authority. "Too much is depending on your success. The Circle believes you can do it. I do, too. So, get whatever self-doubt you might have inside you and get rid of it. It will only drag you down. Trust yourself and those around you."

"I'm only allowed two companions. What good will that do? I need more. I don't see why, if Lucian is this great threat, they don't gather the entire body that follows them to attack him. Surely, we could easily defeat him, then. He can't be *that* powerful." Gessa started to tremble.

"As I said before, the Circle has their reasons for sending you. Now about your two companions, you might be surprised what people can do when they are pushed up against a wall. Trust in them. Depend on them. Guide them."

Gessa's scared eyes stared at Gunthar.

"Go," the librarian suggested and placed a hand on her

shoulder. "You got work to do."

"Thanks."

"Just bring back my books in one piece."

From his tone, she knew his words were meant to say more. Startling the man with a surprise hug, she thanked him again and blessed him for his words of wisdom.

A short time later, after she made sure all of her tears have been wiped away, Gessa joined her two future companions. Her earlier assessment was correct. They were indeed restless. A slightly nervous twitch accompanied her voice as her deadpan expression stared at them. She hoped they didn't notice. "Here's the situation . . . "

CHAPTER THREE

"Can we please stop at the next town? My feet are killing me!" Gavin whined.

The urge to go to Jenna was overwhelming. Nothing could stand in his way, but Nix was not ignorant. Rest would be needed to ensure the trip's success. If they could only find a quicker way of getting there. "Sure."

"We should be able to purchase the horses there," Twyla mentioned as she walked next to Nix.

"Hopefully, then, Gavin will stop his eternal whining," Nix returned.

"I doubt it."

Just then, the pudgy wizard caught up with his friends. "What about me? I heard my name mentioned."

"Nothing." Both Nix and Twyla spoke as one.

"Nonsense. I heard my name. What was it about?" he demanded through gulps of air as he tried to keep up with their pace.

"We were just wishing," Twyla spoke up.

"Wishing for what?"

"Wishing that your gut was twenty pounds lighter. Because, if you don't stop your endless whining, I'm going to be forced to carry your lard ass!" Nix threatened.

Twyla couldn't help but laugh aloud, which only heated Gavin's temper.

"I'm not fat!"

"Whatever."

"I'm not. I'm just . . . "

"Big boned," Nix butted in.

"Yeah."

Twyla laughed harder. Tears streamed down her eyes.

"It's not my fault. It's a family trait," Gavin tried to explain to his humored companions.

"More like an heirloom." Twyla was now rolling among the fallen leaves as she unleashed the full force of her laughter.

Nix had to restrain himself from following Twyla with a fit of his own. Although the three friends have fought beside each other and were associated since childhood, that still didn't stop them from their occasional moments of cruelty. It was expected. Especially with Gavin and Twyla.

Gavin's face was red from embarrassment and anger when Nix patted him on the back. "Easy, Gav. We still love you."

Having vented most of his rage with rapid breaths through his inflamed nostrils, Gavin began to calm down. "You know I'm touchy about my weight."

"Yes, I know. But your face looks so cute when it turns crimson like that." To emphasize the point, Nix squeezed one of the wizard's cheeks.

"Stop that," Gavin waved off his leader.

Once Twyla regained her composure, she approached the other two. Despite the fact that he annoyed her from time to time, she couldn't deny he was a true friend. "Come on, let's get going.

We can still reach Karsonis in time for supper."

When Nix was out of earshot, Twyla whispered to Gavin, "Dinner's on me."

"You're on," he smiled.

*   *   *

The temperature was well into it's nightly decent when they finally arrived Karsonis. An orange haze had been cast upon the small town that welcomed them with the falling sun. Though the town was indeed small, it was no failure in prosperity. The nearby mining operation along with a successful fishing business provided the town with plenty of wealth. They just chose not to flaunt it. No one was quite sure where the money went. After all, the town closely resembled a ghost town. Buildings were in desperate need of repair. The townspeople were dressed in simple robes and tunics. The broken statue of an unknown man completed the picture of despair.

"Feels like home," Nix commented dryly.

Twyla sensed Nix's sarcasm and added some of her own. "Yeah. It makes you want to settle down and spawn a dozen children."

Bringing up the rear, as usual, Gavin inquired, "Where is the inn?"

Gavin noticed that his friends wanted to say something, but held back their words. Pushing them aside, he took the lead. Cocking his head from one side to another, he tried to pinpoint the location of the faint smell of food. Somewhere in this town a slab of meat was being served with potatoes and warm, fresh, baked bread. He could almost taste the butter dripping off of the bread as he picked up his pace.

"Gavin, slow down," Nix said.

"Shhhh, we're getting closer," Gavin responded.

Twyla and Nix shared a quick glance at each other. "Food," they both concluded at the same time.

Normally, the aroma of food only crept into the nostrils of Gavin, leaving Nix and Twyla bewildered. That was not the case today. There was, indeed, a banquet of pleasing and appetizing scents wandering around in the air. The three of them were suddenly reminded of their own supply of dried rations and weak wine and craved for fresh, cooked food.

It didn't take long for the wizard to find the source of the alluring aroma. In fact, only a man robbed of his sight could have missed the large, predominant sign that bordered the roof of a nearby building. *Kym's Keep*, it proudly read with the subtitle of *fine food and soft beds*.

Nix stood and stared at the sign for a moment. Frustration started to brew inside of him and forced him to look a little harder until Twyla came to his rescue.

"Fine food and soft beds." Knowing the fragile nature of the human ego, she kept her voice low enough so it would escape Gavin's ears.

"Thanks . . . I knew that!" Nix tried to bluff her.

"Of course," she ended the conversation.

Reddened in the face from embarrassment and self-loathing, Nix cursed his illiteracy. *What need do I have for the written word? I'm incapable of spell casting. It is a wasted talent a true warrior can do without. A sword and a foe to combat are all that I need.* Nix unconsciously caressed the hilt of his sword. It felt good to remind himself of its presence, even if there are no foes around to challenge. *But, I'm glad I have Gavin and Twyla to help me out in that area of expertise.*

The thought of his two companions brought forth the realization that he was standing alone in the street. His friends have abandoned him. Looking around, the only clue to their location was the swinging of the inn's closing door. Figuring his mind had distracted him enough, he allowed his stomach to block out any additional thoughts and proceeded toward the inn.

Once inside, he had no trouble finding his two deserters. Claiming a table for their own use, Gavin was already drowning himself in ale while Twyla nursed a goblet of wine. Having seated himself in a chair they reserved for him, Nix ordered himself a mug of ale from a nearby server.

While enjoying the welcome taste of the cold ale, Nix's trained eyes took in his surroundings. They contradicted with the building's rundown, outside appearance. Polished oak tables and lively music gave the inn a pleasant atmosphere. Even the people, patrons and employees alike, seemed more alive in here. They were still clothed in simple garments, like the townspeople they first saw when they entered the town, but their demeanor was somehow enlightened. It was as if, behind the protective walls of the building, they could cast off the illusion of dread and poverty and allow themselves the ability to show their true selves.

A lively bard, confining himself to one corner of the room, rattled off upbeat lyrics he timed in with the notes he strummed away on his lute. Twyla, between sips of her wine, wrestled the notion of joining the other patrons who had become captivated by the music's rhythm and dance her troubles away. *Maybe later*, she decided. *I need to get something to eat, first.* No sooner had the unspoken words left her mind, than the overly pleasant serving girl arrived with their food.

Mindful of Nix's equally deprived stomach, Twyla and Gavin had ordered for him. For this, Nix was grateful. A generous helping of steaming vegetables accompanied with a slab of meat grilled to perfection, was served to each of them. Each having been replenished with a fresh mug of ale, the two men dug into their meal. Twyla allowed her disgust for their barbaric eating habits to subside for the moment. They deserved it. Nevertheless, she had to control herself from following suit alongside of them.

"Never have I tasted a meal finer than this," Gavin decided through a mouthful of meat and vegetables.

Nix wiped off the minute potato projectiles that Gavin had spit from his arm. "Nor have I, my friend," he wholeheartedly agreed. "But, I'm willing to bet that it would taste even better if you kept it in your own mouth."

"Sorry," the hungry wizard apologized.

Nix regrettably acknowledged, to himself, that the lesson was not to be learned today. He had to wipe off more food that targeted his forearm.

Twyla laughed and forced a gulp of her wine up into her

nostrils. A brief fit of convulsive laughter made it hard for her to regain her composure. Her friend's amusing outbursts made it near impossible. "Stop it!" she tried to convince them, to no avail.

Gavin immediately called for their attention. Once he had it, he took a quick swig of his ale and tilted his head back. A fountain of liquid that came from his lips covered his face and forced another round of roaring laughter. "Look. I'm a whale."

"Stop it, damn it!" Twyla pleaded. Clutching her chest, her face turned red and she fell out of her chair. The dull thump that proceeded was noticed by all those around her. Pleasant smiles were given to her, by all. All that was, except one.

The exception was an elderly woman seated in a chair near the fireplace. Her face gave no indication as to her thoughts. Shielded by a layer of silvered hair, her eyes never betrayed her true focus. The drunken elf woman went unnoticed by her. Likewise, the obnoxious wizard never even phased her. The object that held her attention was the hilt that presented itself from the other's scabbard. Concentrating on remembering where it was she knew it from, the answer finally exposed itself to her. Fear ignited her body with a start of nervous twitches and shakes. *Could the legends be true? Could Kane have been right all those years? Does that man really possess . . . Great Sarvon! He doesn't know!*

2

The dining room had been closed for just under an hour when the young lad entered. Now that he was finished settling in the inn's three new guests, Kort could go about completing the

55

rest of his duties. He saw to it that all the table tops were free of all the ale rings left by the patrons. Chairs were placed on the tabletops to clean the floor. The dishes had already been done, so he didn't have to worry about them.

As per every night for the past several months, Kort obliged himself with one extra task when he was finished. Having put away his cleaning bucket, he was finally about to spend time with the old lady. Her name was unknown to him. In fact, no one was quite sure what it was. She never talked, but she was a good listener. That was probably the single most appealing aspect Kort found about her. He could tell her anything, and usually did. The motherly smile that she always shined upon him while he talked soothed the loss of his own mother. At times, he often believed his mother had sent her here to comfort him when she, herself, could not.

After retrieving a heavy, woven blanket from the storage room, he covered her up in hopes it would stop her from shivering. She nodded her gratitude in response.

"I hope the blanket is warm enough," Kort began.

The old woman nodded her satisfaction as she stared into the heart of the fireplace. Normally, she would lock eyes with the boy as he talked. Not this night, though. Something was on her mind. Something was worrying her. At first, the boy thought she was suffering from a simple cold spell. After a few minutes with her, he knew otherwise. Attempting to soothe her, he picked up the woman's left hand and lovingly sandwiched it between both of his.

Stroking the back of her hand, softly, "Whatever the

problem is, I'm sure it will all work out in the end. It will be okay."

A sudden jerk freed her hand from his grasp. Clearly, she was in no mood to be comforted. Kort's look of shock brought an apologetic tear to the woman's eye. She had allowed her fears to cloud her mind and block out those who cared for her. She forced a smile to her face in hopes that he understood it's meaning.

"Apology accepted," Kort assured her. "Madam, we have spent many nights in front of the fire. You have listened to me tell my thoughts and worries without passing guilt of blame. You have never turned me away or showed any distaste in our time together. And between the two of us, I have never regretted taking a few coins from my father's box to let you stay here, in his inn, longer." *Maybe I shouldn't have told her that.* "Now it's my turn to listen. I'm guessing that you have the desire to be alone. But, I think you need a friend even more. I may be only thirteen, but if there is some way I can help you, even by listening, please let me. You've been there for me and I would like to return the favor."

The lady gripped the ends of her blanket and pulled them closer. The tears that she shed earlier, when she snapped at Kort, were now overwhelmed by tears of frustration and sorrow. The thoughts of her past experiences and hard-fought battles hit her full force. The lessons and consequences of those long and hardened journeys now came around full circle. A slight turn of her head allowed her to look deep into her young friend's eyes and reveal to him the truth.

Slowly opening her mouth, she prepared to speak her first words since that dreaded day more than eleven years ago. Her silence, at long last, was broken. "Ah cah'k hauk."

It took Kort a brief moment to realize the unfamiliar words were not another race's language, but rather something else. When the woman spoke, he saw the blackened stub that should have been a tongue. It had been severed from her. From the looks of it, Kort imagined that it was done quite viciously, too.

"I-I'm sorry. I didn't know." He didn't even hear his own words as they escaped from his lips. His mind was racing through all those times that she was unable to talk back. What an ass he was. How could he have been so blind to the fact?

Jumping slightly to the woman's unexpected touch, he looked up to see her standing in front of him. His hand was being lifted by her in a gesture that beckoned him to come with her.

No more words needed to be spoken as he rose out of his sitting position and followed her to the room she rented, upstairs.

3

The room the mute woman temporarily resided in was like the other fourteen available rooms the inn had to offer. Small and compact. The bed, which occupied a good third of the space, was nothing more than several heavy wool blankets overlapping each other on a rusted iron frame. Despite its crude appearance, anyone who ever slept a night atop the bed swore to having the most blissful sleep. The woman mentally added herself to that list of people. Next to the bed was a small cabinet which served a duel purpose of a dresser and a night stand. Resting on top of it was an oil lamp that, Kort dutifully noted, would require more fuel soon. Besides the aforementioned, the room was void of any other furnishings. No chairs. No tables. Most visitors passing through required nothing more.

Striking the flint and steel strips retrieved from a pocket in her robe, she sent a couple of sparks into a small container of oil. Instantly, the liquid accepted the sparks and rewarded her with flame. After using the flame on the lamp, she extinguished the small container with a breath, then beckoned for Kort to have a seat on the bed.

Having done as he was asked, the boy watched as the woman pulled out a black chest from underneath the bed and opened it. The contents, Kort noticed, were a hodgepodge of books, scrolls, sealed containers and a neatly folded bundle of white silk. He guessed that the silk must be a robe of some sort. He was soon to be proven right.

The woman's search through the chest reached an end.

Closing her eyes and caressing the leather-bound book she pulled had out, memories flooded her mind. Memories she had not revisited in more than a decade. A quick shudder snapped the memories from her and she was returned to the present.

A look of indecision passed over her face as she contemplated her decision. The moment didn't last long and she handed him the book.

Accepting it, Kort rapidly browsed through the pages. "A journal?"

The woman nodded.

"Yours?"

Again, she nodded. "Weeh ih."

Still not accustomed to her speech impediment, he had to think over the words. Frustrated with his lack of understanding, she snatched the book and thumbed to the first entry. Holding the place, she handed it back to him. "Weeh."

Moving closer to the light, Kort began to read:

This being the year of the wakening, 973. I, M'kayla Barclave, student to the Circle of Elders, leave their protection and, for the first time, journey alone.

Kort reread the lines again to make sure he was getting the proper message. "Your name is M'kayla?"

A nod verified his question. Kort felt better now that he had a name to go along with her. Madam and Miss were starting to wear a bit thin. He liked to refer to his friends and those close to him by their proper names. Strangers and inn patrons were the only people he regarded with generic titles.

A horizontal twirl of M'kayla's right hand signaled the boy to continue reading.

I stop for a moment to begin this journal in hopes of documenting a historical endeavor that will make my masters proud, especially Master Kane. I think I will miss him most of all.

Alas, I knew this day would arrive like I know it shall pass. I take with me anxiety and a sense of fear. My body tingles with overwhelming excitement and, at the same time, shivers with the dread of having to face the unknown.

Megan, my best friend and confident for the past several years, just presented me with a going away present: a beautiful, white, silk robe. The tailoring is superb. It must have taken her months to finish. I'm wearing it in pride as I write this, and intend to get a lot of use out of it, too.

Among my packed items, I have a book of incantations (some of which, I had to copy in the night's wee hours whilst the masters were preoccupied with sleep), a mixture of the herbs and miscellaneous spices and a light pack of various clothing and survival gear.

My journey shall begin on foot. I have declined the masters' offer of having a horse supplied to me. I reasoned that if I was to take in the new wonders of the world, the blurred view I'd get on horseback would only blind me to them. The masters seemed impressed with my logic and wished me good fortune. I think the kiss Master Kane placed on my forehead was what readied me for the trip. Up until that point, I was as nervous as I was the first day I was accepted into the Circle's fold.

I had better sign off, now. I realize I've prolonged my journey's first step long enough. I shall continue later.

M'kayla Barclave

Day One

*   *   *

The lamp's flame dimmed as it searched for more fuel to

burn. Kort closed the journal and fathomed that a couple of hours had passed him by. Glancing at the book, the strip of ribbon that acted as a marker showed him that he was half way through the book already. *Fascinating*, he marveled, *I wish I could've been witness to half the events detailed in here. It would have made for a better life than the one I'm living now.*

Remembering M'kayla, he saw that, in the corner of the room, she had fallen prey to sleep. The guilt of denying her the use of her bed made him set the book aside and prepare the bed for her soon arrival.

Gently, he woke the woman up and guided her toward the bed. Just like the love a mother has when she tucks in her loved ones, Kort did the same. M'kayla offered no resistance and slid under the warm blankets. Her eyelids fluttered as she floated back to sleep.

"Good night, M'kayla. I'll see you tomorrow," and Kort blew out the lamp's flame. With the journal tucked under his arm, he slowly closed the door and walked off to his room.

As he made his way down the corridor of doors to rented rooms, he saw one of the two rooms rented to the three newcomers had light seeping out under the door. *They must be night owls*, Kort supposed as he kept walking. Then the boy stopped. A nagging sensation pulled him back to the patron's door and made him lightly knock.

It wasn't long (in fact, mere seconds were all it took) until the door opened. Standing before the lad was the one who, he assumed, was the fighter of the group. The fact that he still wore his armor supported the conclusion. His eyes lacked the usual glaze one would get in the midnight hour. He appeared focused and alert. Kort guessed he was the type to only permit himself a few hours of sleep because he's always on the go.

"What do you want?" Nix asked as he stared down at his visitor.

The man's blunt question unnerved Kort. "I just wondered if you need anything. I saw that your light was still burning at this odd hour and thought I'd check to make sure everything was fine." Fearing he intruded on the man's wanted privacy, he began to quickly explain his actions. "See, we had a patron, uh, a guest, uh, person stay here once . . . and he fell asleep . . . and left the lamp burning . . . and bumped the table . . . and the lamp broke and . . . "

"Slow down, kid. It's okay." Nix could tell that the boy was scared to death of him. "I don't need anything right now. But thanks for asking."

"Yes, sir." The calmness in the older man's voice helped to soothe his nerves. "Well, good night to you, sir." Taking his leave, Kort hurried back to his room so he could read some more of the journal before he, too, joined the others in sleep.

"And I'll be sure to blow the light out when I'm done," Nix called out and added a soft chuckle.

4

"Kids," Nix laughed to himself and closed the door. "Well, that was amusing."

Returning to the task at hand, he redrew his sword. Never

having been one to wait for inevitable battles to hone his swordsmanship, he continued his practice. The room was too compact for his needs, but that didn't bother him. He welcomed the challenge. It would help to harness his skills for close-quarter combat.

Warming up with a few basic moves, such as parry and thrust, Nix gradually worked his way up to more skillful maneuvers that required some fanciful finger work. Fortunately, he noted, Gavin was fast asleep in his bed on the other side of the room. He was glad the wizard wasn't able to distract his train of thought with shrieks of 'Hey, watch where your swinging that thing' or 'Can't you do that outside? I'm trying to study here!' Gavin's explosive snoring assured him he would not be bothered.

It was about the time the lamp's oil was half depleted, that Nix stopped and replaced the sword in its sheath. The sun was still nestled away so he knew not much time had passed. He fathomed it was close to the end of his watch, though. Not ready to relinquish his position, he lit a spare candle and left the room. It had become too confining and uncomfortable. Paying close attention to the distance he would separate himself from his companions, Nix decided that the inn's dining hall was far enough.

No other patrons presented themselves as he entered. The room was deserted. *Good.* Removing a chair Kort had placed on a table top, he sat it back down in front of the fireplace. The warmth of the crackling wood felt good and prompted him to move closer. As the flames danced merrily around their permitted playground, Nix was instantly drawn away by it's near hypnotic power. *It feels good to finally relax. I can't even remember the last time we were able to actually enjoy ourselves. Always on the move. Always on the run. Is that what we want? Is that what our destinies have chosen for us? Is it all worth it?*

To add further doubts to his questions, Nix stared at the cloth strips that bound the wound on his left palm. Though he was aware the blood was his own, his soul told him it was Bastion's. *Poor Bastion. He deserved better. Oh, how I miss you my old friend. What I wouldn't give to have you steal my purse from me, again.* Carefully unwrapping the blood soaked strips, he wanted to check on the wound's progress.

Caked blood smeared his left palm as it outlining the gash. The bleeding had stopped. Having held up to the test of flexing and stretching without breaking open, Nix decided not to wrap it again.

Returning his attention back to the flames, he rubbed the scar to remind him of his vows. How he would track down the killer, he didn't know. As if awakened from a bad dream, Nix snapped his head up. *I didn't even try. I, we, were right there and never even thought to search around. We should still be there. We should never have left that damn place. My gods . . . we let the killer escape. We let him escape.*

Rage seeped down through his arms and seized control of them. Reaching out, the warrior grabbed clumps of his brown hair as he sprang from his chair and crashed down on his knees. *How could I have been so naive? My friend . . . my friend is murdered and I just leave? What was I thinking?*

Throwing aside small clumps of hair from his scalp, Nix's hand flashed to the sword from his side and swung it around with the intention of destroying the first thing it came in contact with.

"FATHER!!!!" Kort screamed, shattering the silence around them. Then, the boy's limp body fell to Nix's feet.

Where in the hell did he come from?! The sight of the fallen boy released Nix of his rage. *What have I done?!*

People flooded into the dimly lit room before Nix could even bend down to check the boy's wounds.

"KORT!" a brawny man shouted as he raced through the rows of stacked tables, pushing them to the ground. Though clothed in only a simple cloth robe, the man, who Nix assumed was father to the boy, ignored the body and leapt at him. "MURDERER!"

Acting on instinct, Nix's training took over and twisted his body to the side to avoid the attack. Merely successful by a split second, he felt the enraged father breeze past him. Stepping back slightly, Nix grabbed a hold of a nearby table and pushed it back to give himself some more room in case the man wished to continue the assault. Which, he did.

Grabbing an iron poker from its place by the fire place, the innkeeper brought the fight to a higher level. "I'll kill you!" From the way he was heavily breathing, Nix knew the man was in no shape to continue. However, that didn't stop him from charging Nix.

A mad swing, followed by several others, slowly edged Nix backwards until his back was blocked by a wall. He was trapped. The father displayed a toothy grin. They both realized each other's situation. With no room to bring any power of force to his sword, Nix hoped the man had really poor aim.

Raising up the poker over his head, the innkeeper screamed out his declaration of vengeance as he brought the makeshift weapon down toward his prey. Quickly ducking down, Nix heard a splintering crack, but felt no pain. Looking above him, he saw the iron rod imbedded into the wall behind him. Rolling to his left, Nix escaped the enclosed area before his attacker had a chance to react. Clutching the sword in both hands, Nix then prepared himself for the next wave of assault.

The room was now crowded with awakened onlookers. Not knowing what was going on, most just simply stood there as the two combatants went at it. Moving with the battle, the group kept a constant barrier between themselves and the men fighting.

Forcing herself through the wall of people, Twyla stepped into the room to view the commotion. "Oh, not again," she muttered to herself. "Can't he control himself?" Reaching a decision, she quickly exited the wall of onlookers and headed back up to her room. Taking a moment to alert Gavin, who she didn't see downstairs, she opened his door to find the wizard still fast asleep.

"Gavin," she called out as she reached out and smacked his covered gut. The shock of the gesture immediately woke the man from his sleep.

"What?! Who?! Twyla! Go away! I'm trying to sleep here," the irritated man demanded.

"Get up. We have to leave," she told him as she stood her ground. "Nix is at it, again."

"Damn it! Not again."

"Come on, hurry up. We don't have much time," Twyla pressured.

Waving a gestured hand over the cloth sheets covering him, Gavin reminded her of his attire. "A little privacy would be nice."

"Sure thing, but make it quick, chubby." Hoping her insult would prompt him to speed up his task, she bolted out of the door and headed toward her room.

The chore of gathering her possessions only took her a brief moment to accomplish. Simply throwing her few scattered clothes in her small sack and attaching her weapons to herself was all that was needed. With that done, she now had to bail Nix out of another scrap.

Twyla's brief appearance and sudden departure went unnoticed by Nix. He had more pressing matters. Dodging to the left to avoid another crushing blow, he could feel himself growing weaker with every passing minute. Gripping the sword in both hands, he tried to steady himself for the next swipe. He was mindful to the focus of the man's rage. He couldn't bring himself to outright attack the inn keeper. After all, the man just saw his son's body slumped on the floor. On the other hand, he simply could not let the man connect with one of those blows.

"Get him, Wren!" an onlooker called out.

"Show him what we do to murderers around here!" another screamed.

Murderer? Twyla caught the last outburst as she reached the bottom of the landing. *Oh Nix, you didn't.* Picking up her pace, she hurried to the center of the room. After burrowing through the crowd, once again, she now had a front row view.

A quick glance showed her Nix was in trouble. From the way his legs were wobbling she guessed he would succumb to his attacker in a couple of seconds.

Springing to her feet, she joined in on the action. That was, she would have, if not for the strong hands that grabbed her. "Let me go!"

"So, you're in league with murderers, little elf! Well, we can't be having ya help out your friend . . . just as Wren is about to have his way with him, now can we?" one of her captors explained. "We'll just hold you till we see the outcome of this, shall we?"

Unable to break free from the men holding her at bay, she felt as helpless as if she were nothing more than a mere child. And to top it all off, someone took the precaution of laying on the floor to hold down her legs.

"I've got you now, fiend!" Wren announced as the small, curved hook at the end of the poker caught hold of Nix's sword and wrenched it from his grasp.

The force of the maneuver sent the sword skidding underneath a couple of tables, where the hilt stopped abruptly upon striking the fallen boy's head.

Glancing down at the blood gushing out of the reopened wound on his left palm, he muttered a soft curse and wondered if it could get any worse. Looking up, he realized it was just about to.

"Prepare to meet the makers!" Wren warned as he geared up his final blow.

Nix's knees gave out on him. *Maybe, it's better this way. Maybe, I should just let him kill me. I deserve it.*

"Stop!" a voice cried out a second before Wren could bring down the iron weapon on Nix's skull.

The attention of everyone was gained as they turned and looked to the man on the stairway. The flowing robes he proudly wore declared to the group his status of a wizard. "This senseless fighting stops now! Or suffer my wrath!" Gavin hoped his words had enough force behind them. If not, they were in trouble.

"Do your worst, wizard," Wren challenged. "This man struck down my boy in cold blood and I'll see that he dies for his crime." Having relaxed his guard, he brought it back up to continue his vengeance.

Rolling up his sleeves, Gavin recalled the words memorized in his head and spewed out the enchanted lines the spell required. The instant streams of colors sprayed out of his fingertips, he felt a queasy feeling in his stomach. *Oh dear, wrong spell.*

The gasps of fear from the crowd pushed Wren's rage aside once he witnessed the colored streams spewing out from the wizard.

What looked, at first, like a single stream, instantly divided itself and sought out each person within Gavin's line of sight. Nix and Twyla were no exception. Targeting out its prey, the currents connected with everybody. Expecting instant death, the flock of people fell to their knees in mock pain. But, when they noticed the pain was not coming, checked for possible wounds. Like the

70

pain, the wounds were not present, either. Instead, they found themselves in perfect condition. A perfect condition, that is, except for their skin tone. The room was now filled with brightly-colored people. Horrified, the people saw their friends had been stained with various shades of the rainbow. Bright yellow, fluorescent green and dark blue were among the colors present.

A fuchsia-colored Twyla shrieked her resentment. "I'll kill you myself, for this, you fat, bloated, wizard want-to-be!"

"Sorry," Gavin meekly apologized to the enraged crowd.

Not accepting the man's word, half of the crowd rushed forth and ascended the stairs in hopes of capturing the bungling wizard.

"Help!" Gavin called out as he fled from the mob.

"HAH!' Twyla laughed. Still restrained, she struggled to join ranks with the lynch mob as they stormed up the stairs.

Half unconscious on the floor, a neon orange Nix looked up at Wren with defeated eyes. Wren, now a bright red, focused his attention once again on his enemy. "Your friend only delayed the inevitable. Now, prepare to die."

Raising the poker above his head, Wren prepared the final blow.

A hand suddenly held the weapon at bay when the inn keeper went to make the strike. Turning around to see who would now interfere in his attempt to avenge his son, Wren stopped. Standing before the armed man was the small boy he called son. A moment was all it took to realize that this person was not some sort of specter, but a living, breathing boy.

"No, father," Kort weakly pleaded for Nix's life. "It's not necessary."

Forgetting his rage, the weapon dropped from his hand and clutched the boy in his arms. Nearly crushing his son's lungs, Wren showed a sentimental side of himself people rarely saw. Tears of joy blinded the man's vision while he prayed thanks to the gods for having his son back.

"Dad, please. I can't breathe," Kort felt compelled to tell him.

Releasing his grip, he set his son back down and then switch to his 'father' mode. "What happened? DID he attack you? Are you hurt? Do you want me to send for a healer? Is..."

"Father! Calm down, I'm fine," Kort tried to soothe his father's anxiety.

"If you're not hurt, what happened?" Wren asked as he led Kort to a nearby chair.

Having seated himself, Kort went into his story. "Well, I was in my room and heard someone out in the dining area. I was checking to make sure whoever it was, was not attempting to steal from us, like that one time. But when I entered the room, I saw that man in pain on the floor. I guess I just surprised him when he drew his sword. If I hadn't ducked when I did, the sword wouldn't have passed over me, but through me. After that, I guess I fainted."

Wren looked at his son and saw the truth in his eyes. Then, pausing for a few seconds, decided to reprimand the boy. "What the blazes were you thinking? You know better than to sneak up on an armed man. I almost killed him for your ignorance. Now, go to your room and I'll let you know your punishment tomorrow."

"Yes, father," and Kort headed for his room.

"Uh, Wren?"

Turning to address his name, Wren saw three of his regular patrons holding a feisty elf in place.

"What do you want us to do with her?" one asked.

"Let her go. This fight is over," he declared, wiping the sweat from his brow.

5

Only willing to press his luck so far, Gavin opened up the door a hair's width and swiftly shut it back up. The mob was still there. Moving his pudgy fingers as fast as he could manage them, he slid the iron latch back in place. With it secured, the wizard stepped back as if the door was alive. Looking around for a way out, he found none. All he saw was a tiny window that Twyla couldn't even crawl through and the handful of furnishings were either too big or too awkward to use as a weapon.

"It was an honest mistake. Anyone in my position could have done it." Though no one else shared the room with him, Gavin continued to explain to no one in particular. "So their skin is a different color, it could be worse. I could have killed them all. I could have turned them all into newts or something . . . No, witches do that . . . I probably would have just killed them. But are they grateful to be alive? No. No, now they want to kill the wizard." Pacing the room in irregular circles, Gavin fell deeper into his self-contained conversation. "Everybody blames the wizard. Nobody wants to claim any responsibility, so they fault the wizards."

Braving a couple of steps toward the door, he still heard them out there. "They must be deranged if they think they can wait me out. I'm a wizard after all. I can conjure up anything I need to stay alive. I can even defend myself if need be. I can . . . Oh, who am I kidding? I haven't even had breakfast yet. Good Sarvon! I'll starve to death!"

Pausing for a moment, he studied the iron latch on the door. After considering the notion of having the door broken down, Gavin mustered up his strength and slid the small dresser in front of the room's only entranceway. The bed took a little more time to maneuver, but he placed it behind the dresser as a back-up. Feeling more secured in his handmade prison, Gavin laid on the bed.

Thoughts of those outside the door worried the wizard. How long could he wait them out? How long was the spell's duration? Being a wizard himself, Gavin knew of the risks those of his profession faced. Magick was too unpredictable, at times. Sure, simple spells could be cast with ease. The more complex and the more imaginative the spell, the greater the chances of a mistake happening. It took years of practice and dedication to think about conjuring up any of those spells. Sure, they thought of him as the inept wizard. It hurt to be constantly criticized for his many failures. But, magick worked differently for each caster. Each person had their own special connection with the magickal auras surrounding them. Each person adds a portion of themselves to the spell to give it that added touch or twist. That's why it was so hard for him to master his profession. One cannot truly teach another to use magick. They can only be guided and counseled on how to channel the aura through them. Some casters depend more on words and chants while other employed gestures and components.

As Gavin laid in his bed, he thought about all of this. Mainly, though, about the spell's duration. Depending on the words he used he might or might not have made the color spell permanent. Mindful that the only person who could reverse the spell, if it was permanent, was the one who cast it, he tried to recall the words he spoke. Dreading to think of the vengeance Twyla would extract on him, let alone the rest of the . . . victims, Gavin tried to block out the thoughts of those outside his door and concentrate on undoing his spell, if it should come to that. Sending a quick prayer to Sarvon, he hoped it would not be the case.

* * *

"You're bleeding, friend. Let me get something to wrap that up in," Wren offered his former combatant.

Glancing down at his left palm, Nix saw that the red man was right. The gash he made to vow vengeance had reopened. *Damn, will this ever heal? Am I to be forever reminded about my oath? Or is it you, Bastion, who won't let me forget?*

A moment later Wren returned with a torn piece of cloth. "Here, wrap it in this."

"Thanks," Nix said as he accepted the man's gift.

"I hope there won't be any hard feelings. After all, it was an honest mistake. You see, Kort means the world to me and after his mother died . . . "

"That's enough," Nix said cutting the inn keeper off after he finished sealing his wound. Careful not to apply too much pressure on the hand, Nix grabbed the table next to him and pulled himself up. "I'll save you the trouble. I accept your apology. In fact, I would have done the same if it was me."

With guilt still weighing down on his heart, the warrior's words did little good. "Please, stay as long as you and your friends would like, on me. It is the least I can do."

"Your hospitality is welcomed, but I'm afraid we need be taking our leave, soon."

"Are you sure? To travel while it's still dark out is unwise and dangerous. Please, at least stay and rest for your trip," Wren nearly pleaded.

Trying to take that first step, Nix felt his legs wanting to give out. Straining to walk, he refused to let himself be seen as weak. "We need to go. I mean in no way to sound ungrateful by having to keep refusing your generosity, but we are on a mission that I feel we have precious little time to achieve. We shouldn't have allowed ourselves to stay so long in the first place."

"Very well." Sighing to himself, Wren knew nothing he could say would change the man's mind. "Then I shall prepare your horses for the trip."

"We don't have horses."

"You're walking?"

"Until we can purchase the animals," Nix admitted as he painstakingly made his way to and up the stairway.

Leaving the innkeeper behind, Nix walked to his room. It wasn't necessarily pain that made the trip unpleasant, even though it did play a part in his misery. It was mainly because he was physically drained. He felt as if he had just taken on a hundred men instead of just one. That's what was bothering him the most. He'd fought in several battles, but this one was different. Why? He didn't know.

When he reached the top of the stairs, Nix stopped. Positioned in front of his room were about ten men and a very distraught elf. He had hoped that this would have been over and he could just leave. "Okay, people. Party's over. Let's go back to your rooms."

"But look what he did to us! What if we stay like this?" one of the angry townsmen cried out.

"He can't get away with this," another one added.

Sighing, "But, he has gotten away with it. You can't change the past," Nix tried to tell them. "Besides, the spell is starting to wear off." He knew it was a lie, but it was all he could think of to follow up on his words.

"He's right," a voice called out.

Turning around, Nix saw that Wren had followed him up the stairs.

"All you're doing is wasting the night away when you should be resting up for tomorrow's activities," he told the mob. "Now go to your rooms and I'm sure when you all wake up in the morning, we'll laugh about this whole silly episode." Waiting a few seconds to see if his words had any impact, he continued with, "Go on, go."

Reluctantly, the multicolored people slowly moved away from Nix's door until Twyla stood by herself. Knowing her as long as he had, Nix was aware that none of the words spoken had any meaning to her. She was pissed, but she contained it.

"I'll let you take this one, lad," Wren whispered to Nix and made his way back downstairs.

Approaching his female comrade-in-arms, he greeted her with his eyes and turned toward his door. Trying to open it and failing, Nix turned back to Twyla. "Get your stuff ready. We're leaving."

"Fine with me," she stated coldly. "But I get first shot at the waddling one." With that said she left to carry out her order. A second later, she reemerged from her room with her pack and weapons at the ready. "Anything else, *sir*?"

Ignoring her sarcasm, he returned his attention to the closed door. "Gavin. Open the damn door."

"Are they still out there?" an intimidated voice asked from behind the locked door.

"No."

"Twyla?"

"You should know better than to ask that . . . dead man," Twyla decided to throw in.

"Then forget it!" Gavin declared. "I'm not stupid."

"I said to open the damn door! No one is going to hurt you," Nix promised.

"Not with her out there."

"Gavin. We need to get going. As in, now!" Nix demanded.

"I'm not going anywhere."

"Then I see that you only have a decision to make. You can either stay locked up in this room and have me and the rest of the townspeople you pissed off, lay into you in the morning if the spell doesn't wear off. Or you can leave now with me and Twyla and only have the two of us to contend with. The choice is yours."

Nix waited, giving Gavin enough time to ponder his choices. The sound of the furnishings being scraped across the floor told Nix the answer he wanted. Once he heard the iron latch being removed, he barged into the room before Gavin had a chance to open the door for him. The sudden act almost caught the wizard right in the face.

Feeling his strength slowly returning to him, Nix pointed a finger to his friend. "Do that again and I'll lynch you myself."

Gavin remained silent.

* * *

With their gear and weapons gathered, the trio made their way out of the inn and into the night air. By his estimation, Nix figured that they should have only an hour or two before the sun would rise. But that didn't bother him, he just wanted to get as far away from this city as possible, in case Gavin's spell didn't wear off. Judging by his own orange complexion, he feared it would be with him awhile longer.

Upon leaving the building, the image they saw was not

one they would have predicted. Standing before the wooden steps of the inn was Wren with three horses behind him. The horses were just saddled up with fresh supplies in their bags.

"I took the liberty of supplying you with fresh food and water for the animals," Wren informed the stunned trio. "I figured, if you would not accept my offer for lodging, then horses would be the next best thing. Take in mind, I'm not taking 'no' for an answer."

"Then we accept your gift," Nix replied. "Even though I feel that it's a bit much."

"He should get into fights more often," Gavin whispered to Twyla.

The elven woman only commented with a look of death, which shut the wizard up.

"Nonsense. My stables are overcrowded, as it is. Now, go." Gesturing for the group to mount the horses, Wren watched as they prepared to leave.

"Thanks, again," Nix called out.

"Think nothing of it. Oh, there is one more thing."

"And that is?" Nix asked.

"There is this old lady who has a room here. She's rather quiet and keeps to herself, most of the time. I've ignored the fact that my son steals from me to keep her here. Mainly, because she doesn't have much time left in this world. But, she handed me a note with a gift to give you, warrior." Opening up a small pouch from his side, he pulled out a single leather glove and handed it to Nix.

Looking over the item, he wondered why the stranger wanted him to have it.

"She also insisted that I watch you put it on and warn you to never take it off, if you value your life. I don't know what she meant by that, but that's what she wrote down for me to say."

Realizing the glove was for his left hand, Nix carefully slid it on and over his wound. Lifting the gloved hand up, he showed Wren that it fit and smiled. "Tell her I said thank you."

"Good journey," Wren said as he watched them ride off into the night.

*   *   *

Blood ran down the faces carved into the ivory throne and covered the dead man's adorned breastplate as well. The image it had once shown of the entwined lions and looming dragon was blocked out by the red liquid. Flies encircled the soaked remains of the long-dead warrior as it's fingerless left hand twitched.

CHAPTER FOUR

The sounds of the woodland creatures could have been heard for miles around. That was, until the noise of hooves from three horses drowned out the natural orchestra. Mounted atop the steeds were the ones chosen by the Circle of Elders.

Gessa pulled back on her horse's rein to halt its progress. "We'll make camp here," she decided.

"Fine with me," Thomas agreed. After all, it gave him a chance to witness the heart of the forest on a slower, more personal level. He appreciated the speed that the horses gave them, but he welcomed the opportunity to rest and relax, nonetheless.

Like the other times whenever they broke for camp, the three youths knew of their duties. Alternating responsibilities each time they stopped, they set out to complete the work. This time around, Thomas tied up the horses to a nearby tree and prepared their oat bags and water supply. Gessa and Opal headed out into the wooded surroundings to gather fire wood. After Opal had gathered a small handful, she returned to the camp to start a fire while Gessa continued to gather more wood.

It was only a short time later when they finished and were able to relax after a long, hard day of riding. Thomas had the packs open and began portioning out the food supply when Gessa arrived with her final load.

"So how far away is this shrine we have to go to? We've

been traveling for days now," Thomas started off the conversation between bites of his dried beef strips. "It seems like we'll never get there."

"I'm not too sure. I wasn't briefed by the counsel when they chose me," Gessa admitted. Turning her head to her other companion, she furthered the inquiry. "Opal, do you have any clue?"

Putting down her food for a moment, Opal let out a brief sigh, picked up her backpack and rummaged through it until she pulled out the book she was looking for. It only took her a few turns of the pages to find the page she wanted. "Given the information in here, we should be there sometime tomorrow. Is that soon enough for you, Tom?"

"It's Thomas, and yes, that will be fine," he voiced. After taking a gulp from his wineskin, "Is there anything in those books we should know of?"

"Plenty," Opal eagerly responded.

"Like what?" Gessa pressed on.

"Well, as Gunther told you, it was a good idea to research these books and scrolls. According to them, there was this great warrior who built a following like no other. Though the myths of today have exaggerated the truth a little, it pretty much remains true. You see, the warrior's name was Lucian Zharn."

Taking in a deep breath, the young girl closed the open book and pictured the events that she had memorized in her head. "Lucian, in his time, had been a warrior at heart. It was his pride and he chose to master all forms of weaponry. When that was accomplished, he felt that more needed to be learned. So, he turned to the art of magick. Having built a small fortune by performing certain tasks and bounty collecting, he hired local wizards and illusionists who would be willing to betray their oaths of confidentiality outside of their kind. From them he learned many tricks. But to him that's all they were . . . tricks. He wanted to learn more than slight-of-hand and novice illusions. Dissatisfied, he searched elsewhere for the knowledge he desired.

"It was when he met the Master Wizard, Damond Corg, that his search ended. Damond was willing to teach him and take him under his wing. Guided by his new master, Lucian was taught to develop an aura around him and twist it for his own purpose. Years were spent between the two as Lucian's manipulation of magick grew. When the years had finally caught up with Damond, Lucian had all but given up on his first love of being a warrior. The magick consumed his life and he embraced it for all it was worth." Stopping the story, Opal reached down, picked up her beef strip supper and gnawed on a couple broken off pieces.

"Well?" Gessa demanded. "What happened next?" She was obviously enthralled with the tale.

"Let her finish chewing, first," Thomas suggested. "If not, we might have to read those crusty books ourselves, if she chokes to death."

"Point taken," Gessa agreed with a lopsided grin. "Continue when you're ready."

"You two are all heart," the initiate storyteller said, pretending to be offended.

"We try," Thomas said proudly.

Sighing, Opal continued on. "Having received his late master's possessions, Lucian began to research and study the notes and scrolls that he was never allowed to view. After all, Damond was a private individual when it came to his own personal research. For the next few days, Lucian read each one of them and what he discovered in these notes set his heart aflame. They claimed that the world was bound by magick. The aura that magicians and wizards tapped into was not their own inner power, but it was the life source of the world. It was Damond's belief, that when a person of magick would cast a spell he, or she, would extinguish a portion of the planet's life-force. The more spells cast, the sooner the reserve would be spent. That was when Lucian knew he was betrayed by Damond. The elder wizard had taught him the trade to help end the world."

"You were mentioning something about a great following. Where did that fit in?" Gessa asked.

"Not long after," Opal answered. "See, when Lucian had originally came across the information, he held onto it with discontent and disbelief. No way could this be true, he kept telling himself. Unfortunately, the Master Wizard had been right. That's why the Circle teaches us to limit our usage and be alert for any mis-users. It was this truth that sheared the last of Lucian's sanity from him."

"That must have been quite rough on him. Knowing you were trained to betray the very world in which you lived. A kingdom, I can understand, but a whole world . . ." Thomas sympathized.

"Would you stop interrupting? I'd like to finish this story, so I can finish eating my food."

"Sorry."

"Whatever. Anyway, that's when he started up his crusade. Acting out of vengeance for being manipulated, Lucian set out to rid the world of anyone who dared to drain the world's aura: magicians, wizards and anyone else who fell in between. He didn't care if the magick being used was real or trickery. He extracted his unbiased wrath on them all. He quickly gained the support of small groups that were already formed. Though each of these groups had their own reasons for joining him, they all shared the common goal of cleansing the 'dying' planet of its 'plague' known as world destroyers."

"So, how was he stopped? Did the book tell you that much?" Gessa asked.

"Yeah, did it mention something about the sword that he carried with him? I also seem to remember someone by the name of . . . Sasha? Who was she?" Thomas added.

"I don't know," Opal admitted, answering all the questions at once. "I haven't read that far yet."

Obviously disappointed about the lack of further knowledge, Gessa accepted it and moved on. "When you do get that far, let us know. Okay? *I'm* going to need to know this stuff, if I'm going to complete *my* quest."

*Here we go again with the egotistical 'My' attitude. If she keeps this up much longer, **I'm** going to kill **her**!* "Of course, like I'm going to hide it from **you**. Besides, it won't hurt to take a day out to catch up on the history, before we get there. After all, three people can read faster than one," Opal said.

"I'll take it under consideration," Gessa replied.

"I'll take it under consideration," Opal mumbled in a way to ensure her mocking words were not heard.

"You do have a point there," Gessa finally agreed. "There might be something in those books that could be the key to life or death."

"Do we have to read them? Opal is a much better reader than I am. I might miss something," Thomas whined.

"What's your hurry? Just consider this to be much needed practice. Tomorrow, we read. I don't want to be caught unprepared. After you two finish eating, go ahead and get some sleep. I'll take the first watch," Gessa decided.

"Sure," the other two agreed, though Thomas was reluctant to let the words pass through his lips.

An hour later, Gessa had her back up against a large oak tree with one of Gunthar's book opened up in front of her. As the words formed images in her mind, she soon found herself drawn into Lucian's world. Rereading the story she was just told, Gessa felt a closer understanding to the man she was to call 'enemy'. The way he thought and the meanings of each action were made clearer to her. Granted, yes, his actions were horrible and bloodthirsty, but was he truly the villain the Circle made him out to be? All he was doing was saving the world he loved. Was that so wrong, she wondered?

Trotting along at a steady pace, the threesome had moved on. It had been four days since they had left the safety of the Circle's domain. Since then, they each experienced a sort of fear or anxiety as the distance grew further from their home. Uneasy in this alien section of their world, they hid their feelings in their own way. For Thomas, he had all but committed himself to watching and noting everything new around him. Opal, on the other hand, spent every waking moment reading up on history. Though she had to place her trust in her horse's sense of direction, Opal was quick to adapt to reading while they moved along. And Gessa, well . . .

"Opal! Get your damn nose out of that book and tell me where we are!" Gessa demanded. Shifting in her saddle, she tried to relieve the cramp that had found its way into her thigh.

"Of course, oh esteemed master. Forgive my blasphemous ways toward the Circle's chosen one. How may I serve her highness?" The contempt in Opal's voice even forced a shiver out of Thomas. The last few days were not the kind to bind them closer together, but quite the opposite.

"Do you have a problem with them choosing me?" Gessa snapped off.

Thomas pulled the reigns on his horse to slow it's pace. He knew the argument was soon to come.

"No. I just wish they had widened the roads a little more to accommodate your swelled head. That's all," Opal casually replied.

"I do not have a swelled head!" Gessa insisted. "Just ask Thomas."

The two girls turned their attention to their male companion following in the rear. "Well?" they asked him in unison.

"Wow, look!" he pointed off into the forest. "An oak tree!"

Squinting her eyes in a blind rage, Gessa snapped the leather reigns down and sent her horse speeding ahead. Opal's "Told you," was drowned in rapid hoof beats.

Shrugging her shoulders, Opal looked back at Thomas. "I guess some people can't take criticism."

"I guess not," he agreed just to drop the subject. "How much further is it, anyway?"

"We should be there shortly."

As Gessa sped down the hardened dirt trail, she rounded a corner and was soon lost to the sight of her companions. Minutes went by as the two of them moved alone. Neither was compelled to chase after their leader. They both felt, silently, that if their leader wanted to throw a temper tantrum, they should let her. After all, they were heading to the same place. They would meet up again, sooner or later.

It was when Gessa's horse was viewed racing toward them that they stopped and became confused. The horse was moving at a high rate of speed and was whinnying as if it was on fire. The problem, though, lay in the fact that its rider was not present. This was established when the beast shot past them. Nearly avoiding a head-on collision with the wild beast, the young students manned their beasts off to either side of the trail and let the riderless beast pass.

"Where's Gessa?" Thomas asked.

"You got me. Come on, she might be hurt," Opal realized. The memory of their recent argument was lost. It was replaced by a sudden gnawing suspicion and dread. Signaling her horse, she raced forward.

Thomas followed.

Just as the two riders were about ready to hit their top speed, they came to a screeching halt. As if struck by an unseen force, the animals on which they rode abruptly stopped and began bucking their passengers. Unprepared for their horses' violent behavior, the two comrades were violently thrown to the hard ground. Fearful of being trampled, they quickly rolled out of the way and watched as their rides and possessions disappeared from sight.

"Oh, this is great," mumbled Opal. "Now what?"

"Let's try and find Gessa. I'm guessing the same thing happened to her," Thomas replied.

Before they were able to start a search, their female leader walked around a bend. "Could someone explain what happened? All I know is one minute I'm trotting off at a good speed and then my horse freaked out on me," she explained.

"The same happened to us, too," Opal added. "Ideas, anyone?"

"None," Thomas admitted.

Almost as if it was a cue, Gessa paused for a moment and looked around her. The forest appeared normal, yet different. Concentrating on nailing down what had suddenly unnerved her, she asked, "Do you two sense something?"

"No. Sense what?"

"Wait. I'm sensing it, too," Opal announced.

"Sensing what?" Thomas demanded. "I don't sense anything."

"Thomas, feel the air around you," Gessa instructed. "There's some strong magick nearby. Some very powerful magick."

"I still don't . . . " Moving past Gessa, he stopped. "Whoa." Stepping backwards, he nearly tripped over his feet. "Now I feel it. Where is it coming from?"

"My guess is from the direction we were headed toward. That's probably what spooked the horses."

"Makes sense."

"Ladies and gentlemen, I think we found Lucian's tomb," Gessa declared. "Let's see what it looks like, shall we?"

With a renewed interest in their mission, the group headed down the road and approached the ancient shrine.

"Gessa?" Thomas voiced. "What about the horses? All of our stuff is packed on them. Shouldn't we try to find them, first?"

She cast him a look of uncertainty as she took the question under consideration. "Here's the deal. Stay to the road and if you don't see them shortly, head back. I don't want to take the chance of any of us getting lost out here. Got it?"

"No problem, boss." Without another word, Thomas sprinted away from them and headed back the way they came.

"And then there were two," Opal mumbled.

The walk down the road was rather quiet for the two girls. Hearing the crackling of dried leaves under the soles of their shoes seemed to enhance the silence. Brushing back her strawberry blonde hair over her shoulders, Gessa slowed down the pace.

"Am I really like that?" Gessa asked as she stared on ahead.

"At times," the other girl answered.

"Oh."

"I wouldn't let it get to you, though. We're just nervous about this whole situation. That's all," Opal said.

"It's not easy being chosen by the Circle. I mean, what if I screw this up? Then what?" Hearing the words spoken from her own lips, she now understood how the others felt toward her. "Are you jealous that they chose me, personally?"

This caused Opal's walk to come to a standstill. "Are you really that blind? What in Sarvon's name would make you think that?"

"What?" Okay, so she didn't understand after all.

"If you really want to know, I'll tell you. It's not that you were chosen instead of us. It's not the fact that you're older or any other stupid reason you can think of. It's just that we're sick and tired of hearing you remind us every five minutes of your position. The great and mighty Gessa, the chosen one, must constantly keep her subjects in check and always make sure they know their place." The tension in the young girl had finally reached a boil.

"I do not!" Gessa countered.

"You are that blind, aren't you?"

"Hey, you try being the one . . . "

"Save it. I've heard it too many times on this trip. I can't take any more. The way I see it, if you want to lie to yourself . . . then that's your problem. I am here to help **you** in

93

your quest and that's what I'm going to do."

"Sorry you feel that way," Gessa meekly apologized.

"No, you're not," and Opal continued to head down the road. All the while, the tension between them grew stronger.

*   *   *

Panting to catch some much needed breath, Thomas killed his sprint and slowed down to a power walk. With the slower pace, he was able to observe the forest surroundings better. Paying attention to every aspect of the forest that was available to his sight, he searched for his targets.

It was when he felt that he had gained enough of a distance from his companions that he stopped. Peering around to both sides, Thomas shook the tension and nervousness from his fingertips and prepared them for an enchantment. Having cleansed his mind of all thought, the lad concentrated on the words he searched for. After he was sure about the correct structure that they needed to be phrased in, he spoke the words of magick. Waiting for the mystic tingle that was supposed to follow, he inhaled deeply and blew an eerie, malign wail through the cupped hands he had placed by his lips. The sound vibrated out from him and was captured by the trees circling around him. Once the wooden mammoths were touched by the enchanted cry, they acted as a conductor, passing it on and carrying it throughout the area.

Thomas stood still and listened as the sound grew farther away. A smile formed on his face as he waited there.

The sounds of hoof beats told him the spell had worked. The three lost horses were returning to him, as he predicted. When

94

they were close enough, he reached out his hand, and grabbed hold of their reigns.

"That's a good bunch of girls," he cooed as he stroked the mane of each while he led them over to a nearby tree. Afterward, when he finished tying the reign of his own personal horse to a sturdy tree branch, the young boy walked the other two away from the restrained one. But before he left the single beast behind, Thomas passed his open left hand over its eyes and forced it into a deep sleep.

"Come, my beauties. We have a mission to fulfill," Thomas explained to his trailing steeds. Tugging slightly on the set of reigns he held, he passed along the suggestion of moving closer and ceasing their random movements. "Or, I should say, you have a small part to play in my mission."

Turning to face the animals head-on, he placed a hand on each of their foreheads and commanded them, "CEASE!" Obeying the charmed word, they were held at bay. Their eyes rapidly moved in horror as they were forced to remain motionless.

"Do not be frightened. Soon you shall be part of a greater purpose. A purpose that eclipses this shallow existence of life and we'll move onto higher grounds. Though my brothers and sisters from The Order were surprised by his early coming, we will be ready to serve him, again. Lucian shall succeed this time."

As he finished his words, Thomas closed his eyes and concentrated on the animals he touched. In his mind's eye, he witnessed the restrained horses convulsing and shaking. Twitching in a manner that the casual observer would deem as unnatural, the horses' life force drained from them. As if the flesh had morphed into a liquid state, the blood and skin seeped off of their bodies and was siphoned into Thomas's awaiting hands. Feeling the warm blood coating his open hands, the boy grew ecstatic as the spell continued. Tendons that were never meant to be exposed as an outer layer, were uncovered. Like the rest of the outer body, these too were drawn into the boy. This continued until the skeletal remains were all that was left. Knowing the last of the life essences had flowed into his body, he removed his hands and let the bones clatter to the ground. Exhaling a long breath of wind toward the remains, he opened his eyes and witnessed the bones wither into dust and float away with a passing breeze.

Casually returning to his charmed horse, he untied the reign and snapped his fingers to break its trance. Shaking off the spell's effect, the animal behaved as if nothing was out of the ordinary. "Let us go and rejoin the girls. We must allow them to exercise their parts in the master's return, as well."

Once in the saddle, he kicked the beast's side and signaled it to speed toward his naive companions.

3

"Looks like we aren't the first ones to come here," Opal commented as she entered into the clearing. She pointed to the pile of charred wood that was placed away from the area's sole structure: a small, marble shrine.

Without so much as a word, Gessa walked over to the mass of blackened wood and sifted through the ashes. "Yep. That's what I thought," she spoke aloud. "It was a pyre."

"Um, do you think we should disturb it?" It was obvious that Opal wasn't comfortable near it. "Isn't it, like, sacrilegious to mess with the remains?"

"Nonsense. There are no markings or religious ornaments here. Are there?"

"No."

"Well then, I'd say you're worried about nothing. It was probably some traveler who had passed away and was laid to rest by his companions. From the way the pyre was built, I bet you'll find sunken footprints in the grass near its base. My guess is that whoever was cremated here was a follower of Sarvon. It would coincide with their way of worship," Thomas voiced as he made his way into the clearing.

"Glad to see that you made it back," Gessa said to him. "Find the horses?"

"No. I think that whatever spooked them must have gotten to them bad. If I had to take a guess, I'd say it was the aura originating from this place," Thomas offered as an explanation.

"I was thinking the same thing," Opal threw in.

Satisfying his curiosity, the boy looked and soon found the markings that he had mentioned. "I was right. From the shapes, I'd say that there were three of them, one a woman. Judging from the way this set is a little deeper, I would say that whoever had these prints was a little on the heavy side, too."

"This is all fascinating, but we have more important things to worry about," Gessa cut in.

"Such as?"

"Such as all of our possessions. The books and scrolls are lost as well as our food supply. We have a serious dilemma that needs confronted," Gessa reminded them.

"We don't need to worry about food. I can hunt down anything that roams these woods. But, you are right about one thing. The books are lost. If we backtrack the way we came, we might, and I stress *might*, find them. Who knows how far they are by now?"

"True," the female leader agreed.

"If I might suggest, we might as well call the written words a loss. But, we might be able to find what we need to know in that shrine, over there. If we were traveling in the right direction that should be Lucian's shrine. I ask, what better place is there to find a more accurate source of information." Thomas's words were taken in by his female teammates and considered.

"I'm with Thomas. Since we're here, we might as well let him hunt down some food, too, while we try to set up camp in the shrine," Opal admitted. "What could it hurt?"

"Yeah," he seconded. "What could it hurt?"

Puzzled, Gessa wondered in the back of her mind, why Thomas's smile suddenly chilled her bones. Throwing the thought aside, she agreed to the plan and sent the three of them in motion.

4

While Thomas hunted for their supper, the two girls stood in

98

the building's entranceway and stared in awe. Despite the appearance it suggested from the outside, the small building's interior was huge. Huge and trashed. Pieces of wooden furniture laid splintered on the floor. Tapestries hung torn on the walls and fragments of priceless antiques were scattered all about. But the mess wasn't the worst of it. When the two finally got a whiff of rotted flesh, they decided that maybe it wasn't such a good idea to go in there, after all.

Nearly knocking each other over as they ran out into the fresh air, the girls threw themselves to the ground. With each engaged in a coughing and gagging fit, only Gessa kept her 'lunch' down.

"So, (cough) I take it . . . (cough) we sleep outside?" Opal barely managed to ask.

Still fighting back the urge to contribute to Opal's chunky, yellow puddle, Gessa simply nodded a 'yes'.

When their stomachs settled, they both got up and paced around in the clearing. Brushing her long reddish-brown strands of hair over her shoulders, Gessa tried to straighten herself up. Opal, on the other hand, walked over to the edge of the forest and sat down to lean back on a tree.

"I think we might have found a slaughter house, instead of Lucian's place," Opal commented.

"No, this is the right place. I'm sure of it."

"I'm sure of something, too. I'll be damned if I ever go back in there again. I'd be lucky to get passed the front door."

"I know what you mean, but we have to go in there if

we're going to find any clues on how to destroy Lucian," Gessa reminded her.

"You can go in without me, then."

"I don't want to go in there, myself. But . . . "

"Why don't we send in Thomas? He's used to gutting and cleaning animals. He could probably tolerate the smell," Opal enthusiastically suggested.

"True. All right, we'll wait until he comes back. If he doesn't want to go in, then we'll draw straws to see who does. Agreed?"

"Agreed."

*   *   *

It was a tough decision to make. It took him a while to resolve the conflict in his mind. But, after he had destroyed the other two horses, along with the possessions that they held, Thomas decided to use his own horse for another purpose than what he had originally intended. His first thought was to save the beast as an escape route in case things went bad with the girls. After thinking it over, he was ashamed to have considered the option of failing Lucian. So, without a further opportunity for doubt to seep in, the boy simplified his search for food and slaughtered his own horse.

Taking the precaution of placing it into a deep sleep first, so not to create too much noise and attention, he got to work. Using the long blade on his knife, which was magickally heated to cut faster and easier, Thomas portioned out several, rather generous slabs of raw meat. Having already skinned the hairy flesh from the horse's side and using it as a ground cover to place the meat on, he was sure the appearance of his found food could easily pass as that of a deer or another similar animal.

Finished with the task, Thomas rid himself of the rest using the same method he had used on the other two. *At least it wasn't a total loss.* He obtained a long, sturdy branch he found and scraped the bark off of it, and then used it to spear the meat and transport it back to the clearing.

Enduring the seemingly growing weight of the stolen flesh, he pressured to move faster toward his companions. His reason wasn't necessarily because of the weight, or for the need to eat. He hurried his pace because of his sense of anxiety to finally being able to serve Lucian, face to face. That, and the pleasure of presenting him with the first of many gifts his awakening would provide: two, young, female, virgin magick-users.

5

Both sets of female eyes stared in amazement at the vast amount of meat that Thomas had returned with. "Where do you want me to put this?" he asked.

Pulling off the cloth cloak she wore on her back, Gessa placed it on the ground and pointed toward it. "Right here would be good."

"What, you haven't gone in? I figured that I would find you both inside when I came back," Thomas noted.

"See, that's the problem," Opal spoke up. "We can't make it in there. The lingering smell of rotting flesh keeps flushing us out. We can't even stand in the front door without wanting to throw up."

"After giving it some thought, we were wondering if you wouldn't mind going in and looking around for us. Please?" Fluttering her long lashes for him, Gessa laid some female persuasion on the poor lad.

"I guess I could." Fighting back the urge to show his building excitement, he said nothing else. *This is too easy.*

"Great," Gessa exclaimed. " Just remember, we're out here if you need us."

"Uh, sure. I think I'll be fine, though. Besides, what could be in there?"

"Famous last words?" Opal voiced.

"Ha ha ha. When I come back, you just better make sure that you have a fire going. I'm so hungry I could eat a horse," he instructed.

The girls let out a slight laugh at his words.

Thomas laughed harder as he headed toward his master's shrine. Goose bumps rippled up his arms and down his back as he walked closer. *Master Lucian, I'm coming home.*

* * *

Without the foreknowledge of ever being in there before, Thomas knew what to expect of the shrine's interior. Though the sight of the random acts of destruction throughout the building was a little unexpected, it did not phase him. The place was like he always imagined it would be.

Sniffing the air, he caught the nauseating smell the girls

were complaining about. Focused on breathing through his mouth, not his nostrils, he braved the stench and moved forward. He could not stop now. He would not even dare.

As the boy walked closer to the room's center, pushing aside broken pieces of what used to be a magnificent vase with his feet, his mind basked in all the room's glory. *How it must have shined back in its day. I can just imagine the power that Lucian's mere image held as he sat up there on his throne and pondered his next act of vengeance.* Thoughts of wonder and a growing sense of reverence guided his feet.

When Thomas had finally advanced to the foot of the darkened steps, his head lifted up as his eyes followed each step and it was then that he got his first look at the powerful figure.

Blood soaked armor clung to the warrior's bone structure as it sat there on its ivory throne. Though dead for centuries, strands of loose tendons were seen wrapped around the corpse as the red liquid spread over it. Flies swarmed around, drawn by the aroma of death, orchestrating their symphony of buzzing and whirring. As the figure sat there, Thomas drew closer and stared as if he was looking at one of the gods, themselves.

"Master, I'm here," Thomas greeted the dead warrior. "I have waited and prayed for the chance to serve you. My will is yours to command."

Stretching out his hands, Thomas touched the damp skull with nervous fingers. "I bring you a gift, master." Recalling the life forces he previously extracted from the horses, he allowed the power to flow from his fingertips into the limp body of Lucian.

Convulsing as the transfer took place, he watched as the veins on his arms rippled. Replacing the sight of his arms with that of Lucian, the boy watched excitedly as the dead warrior accepted, and prospered, from his gift.

Red veins of blood coursed swiftly over the once dried bone and accepted the tendons and strands of muscles that also appeared. As if the whole decomposition had never taken place, Lucian's body was beginning to take form. Transparent layers of flesh bubbled and stretched themselves to cover the newer layers of flesh for the body. Bones were replenished with marrow. Cartilage pushed its way out of the skin to add form to the blank face. Ribbons of hair spewed out from the head follicles as Lucian absorbed Thomas's gift. Eyes, which had long ago sunk back into their sockets were now staring outwards . . . staring at Thomas. Lucian waited till the transfer was complete.

Dropping down to one knee, Thomas bowed his head in reverence as soon as the last of the stored energy had been released.

Closing his eyes, Lucian leaned back on his throne and breathed in his first breath in nearly two hundred years. Not bothering to brush aside the stringy blonde hair that was matted to his forehead, he relished the feeling his lungs gave and basked himself in the knowledge that, once again he lived. When that moment had passed, he leaned forward and took a good look at the figure before him. It did not take him long to understand what had happened. After all, he was used to a servant's loyalty. He expected nothing else, even after death.

As he looked at the young man kneeling before him, Lucian focused his attention to the room around him. The mess meant little to him. The human nature to plunder and pilfer was accepted and understood. But, as he looked around, a pain in his left hand puzzled him. It wasn't until he saw the missing four digits that he fully understood what had happened.

Like a voice that rose from the deepest crevice in the darkest depth of the planet, Lucian spoke: "WHERE IS THE SWORD?"

*   *   *

Outside, Opal and Gessa had finally stoked a fire hot enough to begin cooking the meat they had laid out. But, as they were about ready to place it over top of the flames, they were distracted by the blood-curdling screams that originated from inside the shrine.

Whipping their heads around, the two girls stared at the marble shrine before they turned toward each other.

Neither one knew who screamed, "Thomas!" first. Nor did they bother to determine the answer.

The small fire and slab of meat dissipated from their minds as they sprinted to their friend's rescue. Pressing on to be the first one to the doorway, the girls felt the rush of fear pump into their hearts. Gessa won the race to the door and swung it open as if there was no weight to the object. Opal saw the opening and beat her inside.

The nauseating stench still lingered when they entered. It tried in vain to drive out the intruders who had invaded the sacred building.

Gessa stared blank-faced at the scenario stretched out before her and tried to search for an answer.

It never came to her.

How could it? Never in her young life had she ever witnessed such a display of raw magick.

The spectacle that held both of the newcomer's attention could have been mistaken by a child or a casual observer for a simple parade of lights, if not for Thomas's screams. Streams of bright red and pale green glowing smoke swirled around Lucian and Thomas, who were held together by Lucian's grasping hands. Gessa thought she saw vague images inside the mist passing around the illuminated bodies. Her distance kept her from reaching a full conclusion.

"What are you gawking at?" Opal shrieked and severed Gessa's fixation. "He's killing Thomas!"

Throwing a darting glare at Opal for pointing out her error, she hurried to the rugged stairway that led to her friend.

The glow around the two magickally encased bodies brightened as the girls drew closer. The more brilliant the light became, the more the men convulsed. The convulsions became malevolent during the next few seconds, as the girls reached the top flight of stairs. Then it happened.

The energy that the magick was drawing upon exploded outward in a volatile force. Both Opal and Gessa flew backwards. Opal had managed to clutch onto part of the ivory throne in time to see Gessa get flung off of her feet and over the steps.

Time slowed down and gave Gessa the impression of

falling like a feather. Five feet back she flew, from the point where she had stood, and had nowhere to go but down. Her body, caught by surprise, was nothing more than a rag doll against the fierce wave.

When the momentum ceased to propel her out any further, time resumed its standard pace and dropped her without pity. By this time, she had prepared for the inevitable collision and wrapped her arms around her knees and pulled them against her breasts.

It did not help.

The impact was bone-shattering. The twists and turns she was helpless to control had positioned her left side to hit the edged steps first. The sharp pain piercing her side ensured her several ribs were no longer whole. Then she bounced and continued her descent.

Though impossible, Gessa felt like she had received the blows from each individual step twice, by the time she impacted with solid ground. Her body cried out in agony and denied her the strength or the power to move from her given spot. Warmth was felt as the wetness of blood caressed the back on which she lay on.

Praising her gods, she was still alive and conscious. Barely.

*   *   *

Back on top of the towering staircase, Opal backed up behind the ancient, ivory throne. She had just witnessed her friend take the fall of her life. Now, she looked on as two men lay unconscious a few feet in front of her.

Knowing one was Thomas, she was at a loss as to whom

the other one was. She did not think he was a good-natured person, either, considering the power struggle he and Thomas recently had.

As the minutes passed by, Opal managed to gather enough courage to leave her hiding place and help her friend. She had to tiptoe around the stranger's body to make it over to Thomas. Kneeling beside him, she slowly lifted his head and tried to revive him.

"Thomas?" she could only whisper, at first. Clearing the knot in her throat, she called his name, louder this time. "Thomas. Wake up, please." Shaking his body slightly, she kept trying.

Perhaps it was her shaky voice that awoke Thomas. Maybe it was something else. Whatever it was, he awoke. Groggy from the blast's effects, he stayed in her arms while his strength recovered.

"........" Thomas tried to speak, but it was too low for her to hear.

"What was that?" Opal leaned her ear closer to better understand his whispered words.

"Kill him before he wakes up. You must . . ." He took a deep breath. " . . . kill Lucian."

Nearly dropping the boy's head from her cradled arms, she stared in disbelief, "That's Lucian?!"

"Hurry!" he warned.

Opal nodded her understanding while she raised herself up. The thought of killing anyone, even a man as vile as Lucian, sickened her. Life was too precious to destroy. So, holding back the urges that were fighting her, she began to roll Lucian's unconscious body toward the left edge of the platform. With the near twenty-five foot drop straight down, she figured this was the best, and quickest, way of ending the evil one's threat.

"No!" Thomas cried out, suddenly. The spontaneous burst of emotion had sapped enough strength to force himself to pause for a couple of deep breaths before he could continue on. "Use . . . magick."

"Magick? Why? Won't the fall be enough?"

"No. He could . . . still survive it," Thomas mumbled. Sapped of his last ounce of strength, he had to resign himself to remain on the floor to rest some more.

Magick? But, what spell? Oh, I hate this. I don't want to kill him, but I don't really have a choice, either, she fretted.

Lucian moved. A weak moan seeped through his lips as he rolled from his back to his side.

The realization that the enemy was on the verge of awakening snapped a decision into the frightened, confused girl. Her middle fingers crossed over her index fingers and she began to rub the fingers together. Shutting her eyes, she recited the words imbedded in her mind to initiate the incantation. The words rushed from her lips at a quickened pace to ensure a faster casting time. The moment her words were finished, Lucian's eyes flashed open with a look of recognition. Her fingers spread wide-open and stretched out toward him.

Lucian barely got out a scream when the swirling cones of searing flames shot from the palms of Opal's hands and bathed him in the living fire. The intensity of the spell immediately covered Lucian's flesh and instantly wiped every strand of hair away, leaving a sickening stench behind. The rancid odor of singed flesh soon covered the previous stench. Opal was forced to cover her face in an attempt to block the smell in a foolish effort to settle her uneasy stomach.

The flames had, somehow, rejuvenated Lucian . . . well, sort of. His soon-to-be-charred remains were alive with fear and panic. The heat propelled the man to scurry around in a desperate attempt to extinguish the flames. When the summoned fire slithered down Lucian's screaming throat, Opal knew he was done for.

Helpless to do anything but watch, Opal looked on as the flames ravaged his blistering body. Tears welled up inside of her causing her to hate herself for permitting someone to die so horribly.

Her eyes were glued to him and she devoted all of her attention to his suffering. This was unfortunate, for if she had been a little more alert, she might have noticed what was happening to Thomas.

When the cone of flames was initially conceived, the panicky girl failed to see some of the magickal cloud of residue seep away from the spell and head toward her weakened friend. The faintly luminescent cloud had floated down and entered the young boy.

Though it was a rare event to have the residue absorbed in this fashion, the boy was expecting it. He needed the power from the magick. He was too weak and needed to recharge himself. Once he finally received what he needed, he could feel the rush that was provided. The slight tingle of warmth pleased him. Soon he would be ready to make his move. He only needed to wait for a few more brief seconds.

Opal's heart seemed ready to break free from her rib cage. Her stomach knotted up as she damned herself for performing such cruelty. When Lucian finally slipped off the edge and plummeted to the hard ground, she was unable to hold back her queasiness.

*   *   *

Gessa was forced to play the part of a helpless bystander as she tried to focus her mind away from the pain. The stabbing reminders from her ribs convinced her that she should just conserve her strength and could get up any minute. She knew the lie for what it was, but it still helped her accept her present condition.

As she cocked her head to the left to get a better view of what was going on up top Gessa tried to assess the situation. She could not figure out if Opal was talking to Thomas, the stranger, or just simply rambling on to herself. Either way, Opal definitely did not look as if she was handling the situation too well. With the way she kept throwing her hands to her face and mouth, Gessa guessed that her friend was steering herself toward a mental breakdown. This was not good.

When Gessa finally witnessed Opal spin around and regurgitate all over the floor, she was thankful it was over. The flaming stranger plummeted to his death. Relief poured through her once she saw Thomas rise to his feet and stared at his hands to insure himself he was unharmed. A smile formed on her. Now that Thomas was helping Opal to her feet, she knew that her friends were going to be okay.

*　　*　　*

Lucian reached outward with his left hand, which the fingers seemed to have gone limp in, and placed it on Opal's back while she remained hunched over. The right hand went underneath her rib cage, slightly above her lower abdomen, and kept her from falling forward. "Thank you for giving me the help that I so desperately needed, young one."

Not hearing a damn word that was spoken to her, Opal waited until she was sure her stomach had settled down. "I . . . I killed him," she said more to herself than to 'Thomas'.

"True, but the lad served his purpose. You did well."

Before she could respond to Thomas's confusing choice of words, several sharp pains exploded on her stomach. Kneeling over further, she saw that Thomas's hand was the source of the problem: his fingertips were beginning to burn through her flesh! "STOP! YOU'RE HURTING ME!" she screamed loud enough for Gessa to hear clearly.

"Yes, it will only be for a little while longer," he responded with an eerie deepening of his voice.

Opal snapped her head up to look at the face of her tormentor and instantly realized who he really was. "Lucian!"

The widening of his grin and the darkening of his brow told her that she was correct. "My dear Opal, Thomas had told me so much about you!"

Wasting no more words, Lucian allowed his right hand to

continue to burn its way through her chest until his entire hand was nestled inside her entrails. Resting all of her weight on his one arm, he then lifted her up to his shoulders and hurled her over the edge like she was nothing more than a simple shot-put. He enjoyed the fact that she was still alive when she collided with the ground, seven yards in front of Gessa's view. He savored the look on her face, even more, as she watched her intestines whip out from her abdomen while Lucian kept a firm grip on the ones he had managed to grab hold of.

Lucian waited until the body crashed onto the hard rocky surface before he released the intestines. The splatter sound it made was priceless to him. Then, after absorbing the warm liquid of life coated on his arm into himself, Lucian proceeded to gracefully walk down the stairs. Along the way, he kept his attention focused on the two crippled women on the floor. He could not help but notice that, despite her own pain, Gessa, whose name he pulled from Thomas's memory, had outstretched her left arm in a futile attempt to reach her friend.

"Opal!" Gessa cried out repeatedly until her lungs threatened to explode. Then she tried to inch closer with her left arm in the lead.

Lucian took his eyes off of the foolish woman and moved over to the black, smoking remains of his former self. The flames had already died out and nothing but charred bones and his soot-covered armor was left. This was what he wanted.

To the normal person, had they attempted to pick up the armaments, as Lucian was doing, their hands would have instantly blistered upon touch. He, however, had no problems picking them up. A thin aura of protection was all that shielded him from the hot metal. However, fastening the iron clasps with one dead hand was another story.

When the last piece of his armor was fastened in place, Lucian felt whole again. Cleaning the breastplate of the ashes and soot, he rubbed his right had over the raised image of his family crest. His fingers followed the edges of the dragon and continued along to the lions until the image became even clearer.

Finished, Lucian hung Thomas's cloak over his shoulders and pulled the hood up to cover his head. Having turned back to the entranceway, he paused to take a brief glance down at Gessa.

To his surprise, she had managed to inch herself closer to Opal. Still on her back, she apparently failed to acknowledge Lucian as he approached her. She was moving, painfully slow, with the help of her feet.

He found it hard to believe that this meager woman was still attempting to make it over to her friend. *Surely, she knows the other woman has to be dead, by now. So why is she still moving over to help?* He pondered these thoughts for a few more brief seconds. *Oh, well.*

Lifting the heel of his boot up, he sent it crashing down on Gessa's left hand. Applying the rest of his weight to that leg, he quickly offered her a grinding twist to crush the rest of her hand that the initial blow missed. Gessa's hellish screams of anguish played out like a bard's melody, to him. It made him more lively.

114

With a tune whistling on his lips, Lucian soon forgot about the three victims he had left behind as he entered into the surrounding forest. His only reminder of the incident was when the dead twigs that had been gathered for the fire snapped under his feet. They brought back memories of Gessa. Each broken twig ensured Lucian that his smile would not fade for a long time.

CHAPTER FIVE

Looking back, I don't think I could ever forget that night.

Though I had been searching for sleep for hours, the bed was still cold. Tossing and turning under the sheets, I had failed to get any rest. I tried to reason out the cause of my insomnia and still remained clueless. The night summer air was not too chilly. Nor was it a lack of proper covering. I guessed it must have had something to do with the lack of Lucian's presence. But, I figured I should have been used to that by now. Since he had found a new love, he had little time for me.

I did not believe, at the time, that it was another woman. I had already ruled out that possibility. I couldn't detect any traces of adultery on him. No faint smells of perfume. No secret glances toward a certain someone during our outings in the day. No, it had to be something else.

Whenever I approached him, or tried to talk to him, the subject always changed or his silence intensified. It was like I was not even there. There was times when I wonder who it was, exactly, that I had married all those years ago.

Needless to say, I soon escaped from the sheets that held me prisoner to my bed. Dressed only in a thin, silk nightgown, I donned one of my robes and went in search of my husband. Though the air inside of the castle walls still chilled me, I just pulled the robe tighter and kept moving.

Along my way down the dimly lit corridors, I exchanged brief glances with the few armed soldiers who were making their rounds. None of them stopped to question my presence. I think that it might have been because they were too scared to. After all, the way I was feeling, I would have laid into them as much as I intended to lay into Lucian and the look on my face probably told them so.

All I knew was that once I got my hands on that waste of a husband, I was going to kill him. I had finally passed the point of being a 'good wife'. I was tired of being ignored and I wanted an answer for his behavior. Nothing more, nothing less.

By the time I had reached the room where Lucian had made his recent place of residence, my bare feet were numb and damn near frozen from walking on the cold stone floor. I was also tired, exhausted and moody. Not to mention, I was right in the middle of my monthly cycle, too. That bastard had better pray that he has some sort of armed bodyguard with him when I found him

"Lucian, let me in or I will tear this door down with my own bare hands!" I screamed before my fist could even rap on the wooden door.

A short and simple "Go away," was all I was given in return.

"Not good enough, Lucian! As your wife, I intend to get some answers out of you!"

Silence ensued as I waited.

"I'm not leaving until you open up this door," I declared.

118

Determined to get my point across, I began pounding on the door, shaking its frame. I intended to continue to do so until either my hand fell off or the door was opened to permit me access.

When the door was finally thrown open, close to the time when I felt as if my hand **was** going to fall off, Lucian was swift to get in the first word. "Woman, I am busy. When I have need of you I will have you called upon. Until that time comes, I have no need of your bothersome intrusions. Good night!" Ending the conversation, he slammed the door in my face and left me to myself in the isolated corridor.

Being a woman, heart and soul, I did the only thing that I could do, considering the circumstance: I fled back to my room bawling out my emotions as I went past everybody. Oh, what a scene I must have put on. I can just imagine, now that I look back at it, how confused the soldiers must have felt to see their queen speed past them like a madwoman. Granted, my heart had been torn and shredded, but having since gotten over that part of my life, I can remember little things that I find myself giggling at, once in a while.

When I sprinted into the safety of my chambers, I leapt on top of the bed and allowed everything to come out as the tears of heartbreak streamed from my eyes. In my haste, I failed to close the door behind me. I didn't care if anyone wanted to witness my crying into my pillow. I didn't care about anything, then. My world was over and I was ready to leave it.

Looking back, I can now see this as a turning point in my life. Before, I was a shallow, timid excuse for a woman. I was the loyal servant to the ego of men. I had shrunk my dignity to allow men to see me as weak and fragile. The way that, I believe, all men see a woman. But, I was finished with playing the part of the inferior half. That day, I began to emerge as a new woman. The woman I should have been from the start. The woman I had to be. Alas, I wasn't able to reach that conclusion, just yet. I had some help along the way.

I had no idea how long I had been weeping on the satin or if I had drifted into sleep for a time. But when I felt the presence of another person with me, I knew enough time had passed to alert the rest of the castle to my condition. There was a part of me that yearned for that person to be Lucian who placed loving arms around me to administer the loving hug. My heart saw past that naive yearning and acknowledged Allena's presence.

She did not utter a word upon entering the room. Nor did she, after making her presence known. She just held onto me and gave me her support as a friend. Sure, she could have pressured me to reveal my woes to her. But, the problem was all too apparent. She was aware of my growing distaste in Lucian's privacy. I had let her in on that fact several weeks ago, when I first felt them brewing inside of me. So, as we sat there, on the bed, she said nothing to me except for the soft coos she whispered into my ears.

"I still love him," I confided after I was drained of my outburst.

"I know," she replied as she held my head closer to her bosom. "I know, dear."

"What am I to do?" I asked in a trembling voice.

"Be strong," was her only answer.

I didn't know how to take her advice, at the time. I still considered myself too weak a person to be facing this kind of a situation. My life was turning upside down. I considered myself to be blessed with everything I could possibly want. I had fooled myself into believing I had the perfect marriage, the perfect life that bore no real burdens of stress and the perfect environment for my, our, future children. No, I had blinded myself from reality. I had none of that. I only had Allena and as I held onto her, I discovered that I still had some more tears that needed to be shed.

I think I fell asleep in her arms that night.

*   *   *

"You're crying?" Twyla asked, half curious, half surprised.

Sitting up from the ground he was resting upon, Nix looked up toward his elven friend and wiped the droplets from his swelled eyes. "Was not."

"You were to. Your cheeks are all red and your eyes are puffy."

"Look. I would know if I was crying or not and I wasn't."

"If you say so," she resigned. "Anyway, it's time for you to wake up. Morning has arrived."

Spreading out his arms, he yawned the last of his tiredness out of his body and welcomed the new day in. From the position of the sun over top of the tree line, he fathomed it to be close to the noon hour. Getting up, he moved around and stretched his back as he tried to get his circulation flowing again. Placing his right hand over top of the sword's hilt that was sheathed at his waist, a gesture that had become more common as the days went on, Nix walked past Twyla and headed for the small campfire.

"You might want to hurry before fat boy eats all of the food."

The tone of the elf's voice was unmistakable. She was still fuming about Gavin's backfired spell. Though the spell had shown signs of fading in Nix after the first day, Twyla's fuchsia-stained flesh was ever present. It had now been a week since that ill-fated day.

"You mean you haven't killed him yet?" Nix asked in humor.

"Not yet," Twyla simply replied. "Besides, death would be too easy of an escape."

"Hey, I'm sure the spell will wear off. Give it time," and he gave her a light pat on the back. "Besides, that's a good color for you."

Glaring at him with a look of hatred, she passed off a warning to him. "Be careful. I **still** have reasons for liking **you**."

"Point taken."

"Good."

True to her earlier words, when the two of them neared the campfire, they found Gavin eating. If not for the respect, or was it the fear, he had for his leader, his stomach probably would have finished off the last of the roasted meat Twyla had hunted down for breakfast. "Hungry?" he asked Nix in hopes of hearing a 'no' out of him.

"Famished."

So much for thirds, Gavin acknowledged to himself.

Passing the leftover portions of breakfast to his friend, Gavin fought down the urge to hold onto the plate of food.

"I'll go prepare the horses," Twyla said, to no one in particular.

"Sure, we'll be leaving shortly anyway," Nix responded.

Having stated her business, the young woman walked toward the three horses that were kept on the outskirts of their temporary campsite. Though her anger with the human wizard was apparent, she managed to calm herself as she neared the horses. Opening up their individual saddlebags, she removed the oat bags kept inside and filled them up with the depleting supply of grain, given to them by Wren. She guessed they only had a few more days of supplies left before they ran out completely. Feeling the tension slipping away from her, she stroked the long manes of the horses as they ate. The presence of her animal companions had placed her nerves at ease, for now.

The two men waited until the tempered female was out of earshot before they engaged in their conversation.

"How long do you think the spell will last?" Nix asked in a low voice. Considering the elven race's knack for keen hearing, he didn't want to take the chance of Twyla overhearing them.

"I don't know. By all rights, like your skin, it should have worn off by now," Gavin returned, in the same low whisper.

" You might want to think of a counter spell before she gets too irate," Nix suggested.

"Believe me, I am," Gavin said. "Unfortunately, I think that might be a problem."

"How so?"

"Well, you returned to your normal self just days after the incident had occurred. Twyla, on the other hand, has remained unchanged. Not even a slight change of color. I think, and I pray I'm wrong, but I think that the elven blood that courses through her veins has reacted with the magick to make the effect a permanent one. Of course, I'm not convinced of that theory, but it might explain why she hasn't returned back to her true color."

"For your sake, you had better hope that's not the case," Nix said as he finished off the last bit of his breakfast.

A period of silence followed as the two men watched the smoking embers and pondered their words. The two dreaded to think what Twyla would be like if she didn't return to her true state, Gavin more so that Nix. Mentally, Nix tossed around the question of how he would protect him from her if that probability should become reality. Then he wondered if he actually would step between the two if a fight did break out. He didn't know.

"You haven't told us why we're going to Jenna, yet?" Gavin said, changing the subject.

"No, I haven't," Nix answered.

"So, are you?"

"In time, perhaps."

"Fine by me. I always like to be kept in the dark." Though sarcasm was never his stronghold, Gavin attempted it anyway and left the subject alone.

2

Trotting along the beaten path of a road, the strong muscles of the palomino horse supporting Nix's weight, they moved on. Joined by it's other two animal companions, they produced a rhythmic sound of hoof beats. The steady measure was a soothing distraction to the restless travelers. Though they were indeed restless, by no means were they conversing with each other. No, they chose to keep the thoughts roaming around in their heads to themselves: Gavin, for fear of upsetting the agitated elf; Nix, because he was trying to ponder why the trip to Jenna was imperative; and Twyla . . . well, Twyla was listening.

As she rode on her horse, Twyla was mentally withdrawn and self-absorbed with the trees. For the past hour or so, the young woman was using her abilities to hear the living wooden structures' whispering voices. At first, she hardly took notice. Too enraged with the crisis of her skin color, she simply ignored the voices. As time passed, the voices were too demanding with their plea for attention and she had no other option but to recognize their presence.

Tugging slightly on the reins, Twyla slowed her horse and moved to the back of the group. Traveling about twenty feet behind the other two, she responded to the fretful trees. "Why do you call out to me?" she whispered in a voice that nearly matched the sound of the windy breeze passing by. "You have called upon me, I am answering."

Evil approaches. Move away, they told her.

"What evil? From where?"

Great darkness. Senses you.

"Why me? What purpose does it have with me?"

Great evil approaches.

"How far away is this 'great evil' you speak of?"

Moving closer. Must move away.

Picking up on the vibes that the trees were giving off, Twyla grew more edgy. Listening further, the warnings merely repeated the vague message and gave her no new information. Distraught, she ordered her horse to speed up and rejoin the others to warn them of the approaching danger.

Twylanna, come home, another voice suddenly called out from the trees. Different in tone and deeper in pitch, Twyla knew exactly who was addressing her.

"Father?" she asked. She immediately recognized his voice, but to hear him communicate through the woodland was a rare and odd occasion. "Father, why? Is it the evil that I have been warned about?"

Hurry home, my little one. There is too much to discuss. Make haste, child. You are to return home, now. I'll explain later. Just hurry. Let the winds grant you speed. Then the words of her father were silenced and replaced by the wind's constant chanting of, hurry . . . hurry . . . hurry.

Gripping the leather reins in her hands, Twyla was at a crossroad about which way to turn: should she pull back and leave the group or convince them to join her? She heard her father's voice and knew she couldn't disregard him. The real problem, however, rested with Nix and Gavin. What to do with them? Should she take them to her home, where no human has ever stepped? The reoccurring issue of privacy and discretion that the elven race stresses to its members put her mind in turmoil. *What to do?*

Between the steady hoof beats and the forest's consistent warning her nerves were slowly unwinding. Facing the heavy burden before her, she chose to accept the repercussions that would surely follow and snapped the horse's reins down and rushed toward her companions.

"Nix!" Twyla called out. "Wait up."

Keeping the same pace, Nix turned his head around to address the elf. "What?"

"We have to postpone our trip to Jenna. We must . . . "

"We must go to Jenna," Nix finished for her.

"No, we must not. We have to go elsewhere. Something is coming and we need to prepare for it," she insisted.

"What's wrong?" Gavin butted in.

"Shut up, fat boy!" Twyla ordered.

"Hey, I was just . . . "

Twyla shot out a cold look to the wizard.

". . . just . . . oh, never mind," the large wizard surrendered.

"I'm sorry, Twyla. We can't turn back or stop now. It's too important," Nix said.

Obviously irritated by her leader's ignorance, she continued to press the subject. "Your precious mission can wait. Something important is coming and it's going to roll right over us if we stand unprepared."

Motioning his horse to a stop, Nix shifted in his saddle

to face Twyla more directly. "What's so important? What's coming?"

"I don't know," she admitted.

"You don't know?" he laughed dryly. "You want us to suddenly stop our travels for fear of something, and you don't even know what it is? Get real. We're committed to something more important."

Waiting off to the side, Gavin watched the argument escalate in tension. Glad he was not a part of it, he merely observed and tried to stay out of it. Sifting through a leather pouch of his, he pulled out a strip of dried beef and chewed as he looked on.

"The trees sense an approaching evil and you want to run off to Jenna?" Twyla threw at him.

"Damn your trees and their warnings! Jenna is too important to be put off by standing lumber!"

"Why are you so blindly driven to Jenna? What's there that can't wait?"

"You wouldn't understand," Nix said.

"Why, because I'm a stupid elf? Is it something that only humans can understand?"

"He never told me why we were going, either" Gavin inserted into the conversation.

"Stay out of this!" both of the verbal combatants lashed out.

"Fine. I'll just watch while the two of you duke it out."

"Thank you," Nix grumbled.

"So, is that it? Am I just a dumb elf?"

"I never said that," Nix stated.

"Then, why do you have to get to Jenna?"

"I don't know."

"What?"

"I said, I don't know. I can't get that cursed place out of my thoughts. Every time I wake up, every time I do anything, the thoughts of Jenna are there disrupting my every thought. It's driving me insane and I don't know why. All I know is that I have to go to Jenna . . . with or without you."

"So you would ignore everything just to go somewhere for a reason you don't even know? Is that it?" Twyla questioned.

"You don't understand," Nix tried to make her understand. "It's something that I have to do."

Forcing back the pain she felt in her heart, she tried to keep her feelings from showing on her face and turned her horse around. "No. I understand. I understand that I have spent too much time with you foolish humans and your blind ways."

"TWYLA!" Nix screamed as he watched her speed of on her horse. "I DIDN'T MEAN IT LIKE THAT!"

"So, what now, boss?" Gavin felt he had to ask.

"I don't know, my friend. I don't know."

*   *   *

How can he be so thick headed? Is it just his nature to be so damn stupid? Twyla kept asking herself. Forcing her horse to ride faster, the elven woman refused to allow the human to bring her to cry. She was made of stronger stuff than that. Elven pride refused her the luxury of tears.

"Father, I'm on my way," she windily spoke into the woods. "I'll be there soon."

129

It took the somber elven woman a full day of riding to return home. Tired from the long ride, she managed to leave the warm, hard, leather saddle and stand on solid ground. Almost instantly, she regretted the inevitable action. Her legs were all cramped up and were stubbornly refusing to loosen up as she tried to walk it off. She stretched her back, too, hoping to relieve her body's other pain.

Looking around her surroundings, Twyla couldn't help but recall an old human adage, 'You can never return home.' True, she was familiar with the area she was in, but there was a strange feeling of uneasiness that engulfed her. *Have I been gone too long? Will it be like I remember it? Will they treat me with open arms or as a stranger who spent too much time with the humans?* Unsure of the answers to her nagging questions, Twyla knew the only way to find out was to get it over with.

A sigh escaped her lips as she let go of the horse's reins and moved toward a small clearing. The horse remained positioned, took advantage of the situation and munched on some nearby vegetation.

Stopping for a moment to reflect about everything, Twyla looked at the clearing before her. How peaceful it was. She tried to justify herself that she was only savoring the moment, but she knew that she was, in fact just stalling, so she moved forward. Reaching out to the two saplings that stood before her, she placed her hands into the few inches of space between them and forced them apart. With the young trees apart, the illusion was broken. The small, open clearing vanished and was replaced by a much larger, more vast community of houses, gardens and miscellaneous structures.

A paved stone road revealed itself to her and showed her the way home. As she walked down it, images from her childhood flashed before her. She saw the fields that she and her friends spent many youthful hours hiding in. The swaying rows of wheat and corn only strengthened the memories in Twyla's mind.

As she passed the fields, the first of her fears was realized. When she entered the outermost border of her hometown, she could start making out some of the residents. Some she instantly recalled, others were still too far away to be identified. Those that she remembered appeared to hold a cloud of confusion about them as to whom she was. But when she drew closer to them, they started to make themselves 'appear' busy. Elven women, confused about whom this stranger was, encouraged their children to move along and out of the way. Doors were being carefully closed as window curtains were being peered through from slight openings.

"Mama, she's purple!" one youth exclaimed to his parent's horror.

"Never mind her, Tharus. Your father is waiting for us at home."

Judging from the child's reaction to his mother's comment, Twyla knew the older woman was lying. But, that was fine with her. She expected this type of reaction. After all, she knew better than anyone what to expect from her elven people. They were a very traditional race. Any change was questioned and approached with caution. Taking all of this into consideration, a fuchsia-skinned elf walking into a magickally hidden environment would definitely be classified as a 'change'.

It was not long before word made its way through the entire community. Elves of all ages and both genders stole a peek toward Twyla as she moved passed them. Questions were whispered concerning the stranger's identity, but no one voiced an answer. A friendly nod was given to each of the people she passed by. She wanted to be sure that they knew she bore them no ill will and posed no danger.

Still, the cold, prying eyes of her fellow people unnerved her . . . slightly. Every person she passed had them. To compensate, Twyla picked up her pace. Though she had been away for several years, she knew exactly where to go.

Placing several blocks of housings behind her, and having rounded numerous corners, the young elven maiden soon laid her eyes on her family's home. The old, wooden building was not much different from the building styles of the human's log-style cabins. About the only major difference between the two was the addition of a first floor comprised of skillfully crafted, interlocking blocks of carved stones. The second, and any additional, floor followed the human similarity of log crafting. With the design fashioned as such, the elven race was able to provide a ground level, semi-enclosed area for a fire-fuel furnace that funneled heat to the upper floor. Though the stone ceilings of the makeshift furnaces superheated that small section of stone flooring directly above them, on the second floor, nobody really minded. They simply avoided trafficking through that spot.

When Twyla stepped foot on the stone floor of her parent's house, she was surprised by the lack of heat she was expecting. Normally, or rather, when she was a child, the heat from the stoked fire could warm the skin even before one would step in the front yard. But, this day it was cold.

Moving through the dimly lite passageway, Twyla went up to the second floor. As soon as she finished climbing the last stone step, she saw her father resting in his chair. With all the years she was apart from him, her father seemed ageless at that moment. He still had the same ol' graying beard she was familiar with. His clothing taste had stayed the same. In fact, she observed, it was as if she had never left at all. It was not until the elder man turned his head to face his daughter, that she did see how time had affected him. She saw it in his eyes. His eyes showed her a lifetime of pain and heartache.

"Father, I'm home," Twyla said, stating the obvious.

"My eyes can still see, child," the man called M'Kunis grumbled as he peeled himself out of the chair he was resting in. "Still, it is good to finally see how the years have been to you, Twylanna."

"They have been about as kind to me as they have to you," Twyla rebounded.

"Humph!" M'Kunis grumbled on his way past his daughter. The man made no secret of the fact that the years have ached his bones. "What's with the skin? Is this something the humans do for fun?"

"It's a long story," Twyla said.

"Then tell me the short version," he told her as he entered into another room. "Make it quick before I join up with your mother."

Not catching the meaning of his cold comment, Twyla foolishly asked, "How is mother? Will she be home soon?"

"She's dead," M'Kunis told her from behind the room's wall. "Five rotations, last season."

Dead? ! Momma?! Twyla thought in horror. "How did she die? Why didn't you contact me?" Wanting some answers to her questions, she stormed into the room her father was in.

"Hey! A little privacy would be nice!" M'Kunis shot back as soon as he saw her. Seated on a round, wooden chair with his pants down below his knees, the elder elf shooed away his intruder.

"WOAH!" was all Twyla said before she made a hasty retreat backwards. *Perhaps I have been gone too long. I forgot where the refresher room was.*

Hearing the rush of poured water flushing waste into a small, covered ditch out in the back, Twyla refocused herself on her earlier inquiry. "What happened to momma?"

"What do you care? She's gone and we have more important things to deal with."

"What do I care?! She was my mother! I have a right to know!" Twyla demanded.

"Who gives a damn about your rights? You abandoned your rights when you walked out on us!" M'Kunis lashed out, venting years of restrained emotions.

"I didn't abandon you or anybody. I left because I had to go out and see why we elves are so cowardly hidden from the world around us. I had to see what was so fearful."

"By the looks of things . . . " pointing to his daughter's skin. "You seem to have found your answer."

"Father, don't change the subject."

"Daughter, don't avoid the issue," he rebounded.

"You are impossible. You always have been. You and your stubborn traditions. Haven't you ever wondered what we could learn from the Humans, Claverins or any other races that share this world with us? Must we be so secluded?"

"Child, those questions are not for me to decide. We elves do what we must to ensure our survival. We have dealt with both Humans and Claverins before and have learned our lesson from it. You know this as much as I do."

"That's not the point," Twyla tried to explain.

"Child, I will not be interrupted!" M'Kunis ordered. Moving toward the stairway leading out, the old elf grabbed a worn-out cloak and slipped it on.

"Father, I . . . "

"Silence! I've heard enough of your cursed curiosity. Your mother saw it. I didn't. She told me that you just needed to live your life and find you own answers. So I agreed with her and let you go.

"It was about two rotations after you left when my dear Shiana grew sick. We were unable to cure her illness. None of our healers had any idea what she contracted." Leaning back against the wall to give him the support to relive the pain of her death, he continued. "Her condition worsened as the days passed and all I could do was watch as she died from the inside out. It took an eternity to claim her, back then. Today, I think it was too fast and wish I could go back and hang on to those last precious   moments.

"When she did leave, your brothers and I tried to find you. The trees had failed to locate you. I lost track of all of the days I spent trying to talk to you," he informed her.

Five rotations? The trees couldn't find me? Of course, I was in the mountain ranges . . . where Derek had died, Twyla realized.

"I feared your mother would see you in the *Great Passing* when she arrived, herself. Worried, your brothers went out to see what had happened to you. To this day, they have yet to return. So, thanks to your desire to leave your people, I also lost the rest of my family and was left alone." When he was finished, M'Kunis straightened himself up and looked in his daughter's eyes without a tear on his face. The old elf was all dried out of them.

"Is that why the fire below is unlit?" She had no idea why she asked that, of all of the questions or comments that came to mind. But, nevertheless, she did.

"A man who's dead inside needs no warmth," he plainly answered.

"I-I didn't know. Oh, Father, I'm so sorry. I didn't know," Twyla said, sobbing the tears her father denied himself. Wanting to embrace the somber man with an affectionate hug, she moved toward him.

"Of course, you didn't know. You were out screwing humans, instead. Now come on, you have a mess you need to clean up." Then, he left Twyla alone, as he was, and headed down the stairs leading out.

4

Twyla followed her father down the streets of the village. Actually, it would be more accurate to say she was following his shadow. As they moved along, Twyla stayed a few feet behind the grumpy man and was patient to find out where she was being led to.

The words M'Kunis had thrown at her hurt. They confused her as well. Why was he so concerned when he talked to her in the woods? Why did he call out to her after all these years? She would have given anything to know more about these questions. Perhaps, in time, she will.

As she walked, her thoughts were also taken up by images of Nix. *How could he be so obsessed with Jenna? He's been acting so weird since Bastion's death. It's like he's not the same person I once knew. He seems more withdrawn and ascetic lately. Okay, maybe not so ascetic, but he's definitely changed. I wonder if Bastion's death caused more damage than he lets on. Then again, maybe there is something else that I haven't been able to pick up on, yet.* Twyla paused for a second and considered her thoughts. *Wait a minute, what if it wasn't Bastion? What if it was the shrine and that sword he picked up? Gavin felt a powerful magick at work there, could the sword be a part of it? Its mere appearance strongly suggests a magickal origin. But, what does it have to do with Jenna? Damn, I wish Nix was here so I could ask him.*

"Twylanna!"

Hearing her name called out, Twyla realized that she had stopped in the middle of the street, entranced in her thoughts. "Huh?"

"Are you coming?" her father asked impatiently.

"Sorry, I'm coming."

"Good, we're almost there."

"Where are we going, anyway?" she asked as she moved to catch up.

"You need to talk to Kelvin. He's our historian, in case you forgot during your absence."

"I know who he is. I haven't been gone that long."

Not bothering with another response, M'Kunis continued to walk to Kelvin's house.

When they finally arrived, M'Kunis gave a swift knock on the second floor door after they went through the first floor tunnels. Listening to the movement of shuffling feet, they soon saw the door open up to them. A middle-aged elf greeted them and welcomed them into his home.

"I've been expecting the two of you. Please come in."

Accepting the offer, Twyla and her father entered the man's home. "Please, have a seat. We have much to talk about," Kelvin told Twyla.

"Now that you're here, I'll be going." M'Kunis said. "I've other things to do."

"Of course, sir. Thank you for bringing her here," Kelvin said, expressing his gratitude.

M'Kunis grumbled something about foolish girls and nosy interlopers as he headed back down the stone stairway and back to his own house. Neither Twyla nor Kelvin fully heard what the elder man said and were probably glad that they didn't.

"I'm sorry about that. He hasn't been the same since your mother passed away," Kelvin apologized.

"So I gathered."

"I'm guessing you want to know why you're here?"

"There was something about an approaching evil mentioned. You can start there."

"In good time, but first off, I'm the one who told your father to contact you. I told him little as to why I wanted to see you. In fact, nobody in the village is aware of what is coming. Tonight I am preparing to address the council and let them know," Kelvin explained.

"Let them know what?" Twyla asked.

"First things first. I have to ask you some questions. Okay?"

"Fine. Ask away."

"You and your companions, the warrior, thief, and wizard, had found a shrine, right?" he asked.

"How do you know about them?"

A smile was the only answer she would receive, "The answer, please?"

"Yeah, Gavin was commenting about how strong the magick aura was there."

"That's what I thought. When you went in the building, did you find something . . . unusual? Something odd?"

"The building's inner layout was rather huge. It had to be magickally enhanced. The outer layer could not have held that much space."

"Anything else?" Kelvin asked.

"There was a throne with a skeletal warrior resting on top of it. Why?"

Ignoring the question, Kelvin continued to ask questions of his own. "Was there a sword with the skeleton?"

"Yeah. Nix found it."

"He didn't remove it, did he?" the historian pried as he leaned closer in his seat, toward Twyla.

"Yes, as a matter of fact, he did. Why?" Twyla could hardly contain her curiosity.

"Then the dreams I've been having are true," was all Kelvin answered her with.

"What dreams? Stop speaking as if I wasn't even here and tell me what you're talking about." Now she was getting mad.

"Sorry. I get carried away, at times. I keep forgetting that most people have a hard time following what I have to say. It's just that something of this magnitude hasn't been seen for the last couple of centuries. It's really astonishing, when you stop and think about it. I even have a hard time . . . "

"Kelvin!" Twyla screamed.

"Sorry."

"Just tell me, as simply as possible, what it is that is so spectacular."

"Well . . . " Kelvin started out. "Spectacular wouldn't be the word I would have chosen." He quickly continued when he saw Twyla's mood worsening. "You and your friends have awakened a sleeping evil. When your teammate removed the sword, he broke an ancient spell that had kept the evil at bay for the last three hundred years. Also, you're particularly at fault."

"Me? How?" It was now Twyla's turn to lean closer to Kelvin.

"About three hundred years ago, there once walked a man, if you want to call him that, who went by the name of Lucian. The skeletal warrior you saw . . . that was him." Stopping for a second, he took in a deep breath. "As far as your role in releasing him . . . it wasn't really your fault, consciously, that is. When you found the clearing, hidden from all eyes but elven, the magick concealing the area was immediately broken when your human friends were led through it. Elven magick hid Lucian's shrine from those searching for it. Now, it can welcome all passers-by."

"Hey, I didn't know about it," Twyla said in defense.

"Nor were you meant to, the terror he shed was bloodcurdling and his location needed to be secret. You see, this man was possessed with greed and a thirst for power. There are those who would probably disagree with me, but I personally believe he carried a great fear with him, too. Not for those who were fearful of him, but he being fearful of everybody else."

Twyla raised a single eyebrow, stating her confusion.

"Hold on. All will be clear in a minute."

"I hope so."

"Trust me," he told her. "The reason I said that was because of the actions he carried out. When the name of Lucian was first beginning to spread across the countryside, his actions were random, unpredictable and seemingly without meaning. It wasn't until his power grew to heights that nobody expected that people took the time to see what he was really doing."

"Which was?" Twyla interrupted.

"Something I'll never get to, if you don't stop interrupting. Anyway, it was soon found out that he was crusading to banish magick and destroy all the users there of. He didn't care if it was a con man using sleight of hand or a wizard casting a spell of fire. They were all targets for his wrath. He had sensed and sought out all forms of magick to destroy it. His quest brought much confusion and fear throughout the lands. People tried to hide and run from him, but he always managed to find them.

"The part that most folks missed when they tried to figure him out was that he, himself, was using magick to do this. The great destroyer of magick was hoarding all the power for himself. He wasn't out killing for vengeance, as most of the books read. He was eliminating the competition. He figured that if he was the sole bearer of magick, no one could stop him. That's why I mentioned the fear. I think he was afraid that anyone else who held onto the power could destroy him," Kelvin explained.

142

"But, he was stopped," Twyla said.

"Yes. Yes, he was. The irony of it all was that he was partially responsible for his own fall." Shifting in his seat to get a more comfortable position, Kelvin poured himself a cup of water and then continued. "Before Lucian struck his first kill, he had cast a spell of his own creation that shielded him from all harm. 'No man could inflict damage upon him.' Any wounds would heal the instant it was made. So you might as well say he was near immortal.

"That spell was the first of his three fatal mistakes. He had concocted a spell that prevented him to be killed by any man . . . but not a woman. His arrogance blinded him and he fathomed that the only person who could threaten him was a man. Women were inferior to him. So his male ego prevented him from discovering this particular weakness.

"Considering he was first a weapons master, Lucian also had a special sword forged to help increase his power," Kelvin revealed.

"The sword that Nix found," Twyla came to realize.

"Exactly. The sword was fashioned with an enchantment that greatly diminished the minimal of his enemies. Even I do not know the true extent of its power, though I suspect it has something to do with blood. By whatever means, the more damage he dealt out with that sword, the more powerful he became. But, the sword did play a key part in his downfall. Like I said, he made three fatal mistakes and this was the second one. The third one was his . . ." and he stopped. Closing his eyes, he seemed to be in a deep thought.

"His what?" Twyla demanded.

"You've got company outside the town's perimeter. It would appear that your friends are looking for you. I can finish this later. You should go see them."

"How do you know this?" she questioned. "What foresight do you possess that should make me even believe a word of what you have said?"

"Of course, young Twyla, you always were the skeptic. Allow me to explain myself. My duties are a sacred one. The title of Historian holds more to it than most would fathom. You see, it is my duty to record and witness everything that deals with the elven race. From whenever a child, such as you were, takes her first step, to every brief random encounter we elves have with an outside race, I know and see it all. Most of my knowledge appears in the form of a dream or what most see as a daydream or vision. I cannot control or block out the knowledge I am to receive. When it comes, it comes, and I remember it until I am able to write it down.

"Though you might not remember me from your childhood, I was present for it, as I was with most others including your father, his father, and even his father. My job has consumed many years of my life, but has granted me so many more. As you're well aware, the normal elf can live as much as two and a half centuries, I am destined to live through ten of them. At the turn of the century, I will finally be graced with my death and another shall fill my spot," Kelvin went on to explain.

"But, you are elven, are you not?" Twyla had to ask.

"Of course, I am. Only an elf can hold this position."

"Well, then, since you have all of this information about Lucian, why don't you go out and deal with him? Why even talk to me?" Twyla asked.

"I am forbidden. My duty is to record history, not make it. You could not imagine the consequences that would occur if I did and I have no intention to explain them to you, now. So don't ask," Kelvin told her.

"But, by telling me all of this, haven't you broken your vow already?" She pointed out.

"No. Not really. I have not interfered past my required point. After all, what is the point of owning the knowledge if you cannot share it? I am able to warn, tell or reveal any bit of information that I choose to. I am just restricted from becoming an active participant."

"I see."

Stretching out of his chair, Kelvin walked his cramped legs around the room. "I have no more time to explain things to you. You need to go to your friends before they move out any farther. You're going to need their help."

Twyla gave a silent nod and gave Kelvin a slight curtsy to show her appreciation as she walked toward the door. *Why do I have the feeling of wishing I had never left the village in the first place?*

5

"Are you sure that you saw her come this way?" Nix asked Gavin for probably the fifth time since they began their attempt to catch up with their fled companion.

Drudging out the same answer, for the equal number of times, Gavin grumbled, "Yes."

"Positive?"

"For the love of Sarvon, will you just accept my answer for what it is?! Listen to me, with your non-believing ears, for I shall not repeat myself any further. I said I saw her going this way and that means I saw her going this way," Gavin exclaimed. Enforcing his statement, the overweight wizard signaled his horse to bypass his leader.

"No need to get all worked up, Gav. It was just a question."

"But it is a question I grow tired of hearing. Considering the facts, we should have already made it into the next town or at least set up camp. If you two wouldn't have had your little lovers' quarrel, I wouldn't be starving right now," Gavin said.

"It wasn't a lover's quarrel," Nix declared as he moved side by side with Gavin.

"Nix, I'm not a fool. I do have eyes, you know."

"Then your eyes have been lying to you. Me and Twyla are just friends. That's all and nothing more."

Gavin couldn't help but let the snicker that had built up escape his lips.

"It's not funny."

"Perhaps it's not my eyes that lie, but yours, my friend. Nix, we've been friends long enough that I feel I can speak frankly with you."

"But . . . "

"Hold on. I'm not finished," Gavin intervened. "I know the two of you haven't been intimate, but there is no mistaking the love you each have for the other. I see it when you talk to one another and in the way you both steal longing glances when the other's back is turned. Besides, if both of you weren't so damn self-reliant, you might be able to make something of it."

Nix was silent when he stopped and dismounted. He tried to occupy himself by rummaging through his saddlebag, but no matter how hard he tried, he couldn't stop himself from looking into Gavin's probing eyes. "It could never work," he finally admitted, more to himself that toward Gavin.

"Why not?" the wizard asked, slightly exasperated. "You're bullheaded. She's bullheaded. She's stubborn. You're stubborn. Face it, you're perfect for each other." Then he too, came to a stop, but decided to stay mounted on his horse.

The two stayed silent as the next few minutes passed. Gavin watched as Nix wandered around with his head held down. *Did I overstep my boundary?* he asked himself. *No, I don't think I did. Maybe it was something I should have done years ago, before Derek came into the picture. Dammit, why do I have to get stuck in the middle of this crap? It's not like they need me around, anyway. Every time I go to cast a spell, or do anything else for that matter, it always backfires on me. Perhaps I should follow Twyla's lead and go off on my own, too.*

Though his head was down and the words Gavin spoke repeated constantly in his head, Nix tried to focus on the task at hand: finding Twyla's trail again. Now, he had to start over from the beginning.

Searching the ground for signs of hoof prints, or trampled blades of glass, to show that the elf and her horse passed through this area, Nix fought with his conscience to force back thoughts of Twyla and their last conversation. *How could she leave me like that? She knows how important it is to get to Jenna.* (BUT, WHY?) *I don't know. I just feel that it's the right thing to do.* (DO YOU?) *Well, I . . . I'm . . . I think . . . No, of course I do. I have to go there. Something is telling me that, if I don't, something horrible will happen.* (AND HER LEAVING WASN'T HORRIBLE ENOUGH FOR YOUR BLEEDING, JUVENILE HEART?) *It's not like that. We're just friends.* (LIAR) *Am not!* (ARE, TOO) *Am not!* (SEE YOU *ARE* BEING JUVENILE) *Leave me alone.* (ADMIT IT) *I said leave me alone!* (AND I SAID ADMIT IT) *What do you want from me?* (TO ADMIT THE TRUTH TO YOURSELF) *I can't. It's not right.* (STOP THE BULLSHIT AND LET IT OUT!!!)

"All right, I admit it! I love her dammit and I can't bring myself to stare her in the face and let her know how I feel. Now, leave me alone!" Nix screamed out loud to the voice pestering his mind.

"Fine," Gavin replied defensively. "I won't bring it up again."

Nix shot a quick look toward his friend and suddenly realized what he had done. "Sorry. I didn't mean that. That woman just drives me crazy and I just can't help loving her for it. Sounds stupid, huh?" he tried to explain as he massaged his temples.

"Forget it. It was my fault for bringing it up in the first

148

place," Gavin said in an attempt to place the blame on himself.

"Gavin, don't," Nix said. "If you did anything, it was helping me sort through my feelings. I get a bit defensive when I have my guard down, like that."

"Water under the bridge?" Gavin asked hopefully.

"Water under the bridge," the warrior confirmed.

Sealing their words, the two shook hands and then continued to scan for clues to Twyla's whereabouts. Gavin remained on his steed, looking around from a higher level of view. All the while, Nix wanted to keep a closer look and stayed on the ground.

"Nix?" Gavin asked shyly.

"Yeah?"

"I know we've been through this before, but now that it's just the two of us, why are we going to Jenna?"

Sighing away the shudder he felt approaching him, Nix thought through the words he wanted to say. "I don't know. I don't know if I can even explain it."

"Oh."

"Have you ever had the urge to do something that, for no particular reason, you had to do? No matter how simple that urge had been."

"I think so. There was a time when I had a sudden craving for one of my mother's homemade stews, years after she passed on," Gavin answered. "Something like that?"

"Kind of, but not really. See, there's something telling me that I, or we, have to be in Jenna. I even get this slight sickness in my stomach, if I detract from that train of thinking. It's nothing I can control."

"Do you think it might have something to do with distancing yourself from Bastion? I mean, you were really shook up about his death."

The mere mention of Bastion's name chilled Nix's bones. *Great Sarvon, I forgot about Bastion! How could that vow slip from my mind? Am I that consumed with getting to Jenna? What's wrong with me?*

"....that sword."

"What?" Nix asked as he snapped out of his trance.

"I said, you haven't been yourself since you took possession of that sword," the wizard repeated.

"Leave the sword out of this," Nix warned. Unconsciously, he also grabbed ahold of the sword's hilt as he stood firmly before his friend.

"If only you could step outside of yourself to see how much you have changed. You never been this . . . confused."

"I'm not confused and the sword has nothing to do with it," Nix replied more defensively.

"What is it with that sword? You're always playing with it or, at least, gripping the hilt."

"What do you have against it? It's just a sword," Nix demanded irritably.

"Just a feeling, I guess. Call it wizard's intuition. You know, it's not something I can grasp. Like you and your quest for getting to Jenna," he explained with a cocky air around his voice.

"You're paranoid when you should be searching for Twyla."

150

Turning his back, he left the conversation unfinished. "Now, keep looking. If we can't pick up her trail soon, we'll leave her to herself and carry on. If she wants to find us later, then she will have to do the searching."

"If that's what you want to do." Gripping the leather reigns tightly in his hands, the hefty magick-user tugged to the left and turned his horse around. Attempting to avoid any further conversation glitches, he circled around the open plain they stopped in.

From Nix's point-of-view, the forest seemed barren, save for the occasional rustling of leaf-endowed branches or a soft bird song. He also took into account the blackness that was starting to weave throughout the living structures like finely woven cloth. Soon the moon's rays would be the only thing saving them from the dark void of night.

"I think we better set up camp," Gavin suggested without averting too much attention back at Nix.

"Works for me."

6

All I have to say is, if he expects an apology out of me, I'm going to ram an arrow up his ass, Twyla swore to herself.

Marching down past the village square, she let her frustration push her pace faster. With the grinding of the road-lining stones under her boots, she ignored her people's prejudice glares.

Before she had set foot into her home village, she had not

truly been bothered by her new pigment, until now. It hurt her that her own race, of all people, should make her feel this way. Granted, she was still furious with Gavin for placing her in this predicament. However, the past is sealed and tomorrow will hopefully grant her more power to accept it.

As she moved through the worn streets, she allowed the anger she felt toward her people's ignorance to feed her frustrations with Nix. In addition, from her standpoint, she knew if she wanted to catch up with the two buffoons, she would have to hurry before it got any darker.

CHAPTER SIX

The once-warm blood had long since caked her long, charcoal-black strands of hair to her face as she dropped her head to the hard, cold ground. It helped her to keep focused. The pain had a way to remind her that she was still alive. How? That was beyond her, but somehow Gessa survived Lucian's wrath.

The torn strip of cloth wrapped around her head had soaked up its limit in blood and was allowing some to seep into her eyes. Still, she didn't care. She had been like this for the past two days.

Forcing herself back up, she only managed to make it to her knees. Oh, how they hurt, too. Her cloudy memory of recent events could not recall when the cloth layer of her leggings had worn through. She only wished she still had them to cover her swollen, infected knee caps.

Flashes of Opal and Thomas passed before her remembering eyes. The screams would be following next, she knew. They always were. How quick it all happened, too.

But, screams were what initiated the events she hazily recalled. Thomas's screams, to be exact. To hear a woman scream was one thing. To hear a man break down into wails of terror, well, that had a way of making the mightiest of warriors cringe. That is what happened, though.

Facing the hard truth of moving forward or stopping to die

where she laid, Gessa found the strength to support herself enough to manage a crawling position. Lacking the fortune of having both arms to use, as the bones in her left wrist had been shattered early on during the brief struggle, she used the right on which to move forward. The pain was excruciating, like the cracked ribs threatening to poke through her side. Inching slowly down a traveling road she had stumbled upon, she fought for consciousness. The thought of opting for the tranquillity that death would provide appeared, then faded as quickly as it had arrived. No! No, she had to survive. She had to stop him. She had to kill Thomas.

CHAPTER SEVEN

Rain pelted down on the small town of Karsonis. It was typical during this time of year, before the autumn climate kicked in. This time, though, it brought a new element to cast upon the town.

A lone man stood and watched the small lights flooding out of the buildings flicker and fade from atop of a nearby hill that overlooked the entire town. Observing the habitat with uncaring and judgmental eyes, he waited.

Water had long since weighed down his clothes, making the iron breastplate underneath his cloak seem even heavier. He would have noticed, if his mind was not elsewhere.

Flexing his hands, he simply stood there. The left hand was giving him trouble. The fingers were inoperative, with only the thumb willing to move. When he acquired this new body, he never figured he'd keep some attributes from the old one.

Running his left, limp fingers through his sandy blonde hair, the man barely gave a thought to the naive, young boy named Thomas, whom he had stolen it from. Now Lucian resided inside and he already had plans on using his new lease on life.

The sword has passed through here, Lucian thought. *Its trail is weak, but unmistakable. Perhaps there are only a few days separating our arrivals. The answers will be in this village. Then I'll find the thieves who stole her from me.*

Snapping his head sharply to the left and then to the right, Lucian cracked the bones in his neck and swiftly followed up with the first step that would lead him into the small, sleeping town.

2

The ominous sound of silence followed Lucian the moment he entered the outskirts of Karsonis. He made no attempt to hide his presence. It was the area that had quieted itself. Small animals scurried out of the way to make a clear path.

Throughout all of the town's buildings, the only light (or sound, for that matter) transpired from one building: *Kym's Keep*. Sounds of drunken camaraderie, mixed in with tunes from a lyre, poured through the swinging doors. This was where Lucian headed first.

*   *   *

Twisting around the crowded tables, Tiana prayed she could keep her tray, heavy with sloshing mugs of ale, steady. She hated her job. Being paired that night with only one other girl to help her out, she yearned for the comfort of her bed.

It had been a long day. Between the rude and pathetic patrons and the maddening racket Lyn was producing with his music, she was reaching the ends of her limits. But, she kept reminding herself, the money was good. Especially from the drunken ones. They were unable to comprehend how much they were tipping or, simply, they were more carefree with their money. Anyway, she didn't care what the reason was. It was the only thing that kept her going.

"Hey, sweet thing! Could you hurry up? I'm dying of thirst over here," someone called out to her from across the room.

"Die then, Rhon. Just make sure you leave your purse," Wren, the inn's owner and bartender, shouted back from behind his counter.

Tiana could hear Rhon's drinking partners roar their laughter. Too bad they thought he was joking. She knew Wren only tolerated Rhon because of his steady patronage.

Continuing on, she reached her table of destination and began to off-load the requested beverages. That was when she found out her night was going to get longer and her bed seemed impossibly far away.

Out of the corner of her eye, she saw the entrance doors swing open. Between the two hinged pieces of wood stood a young man who stayed paused there. No one seemed to mind him joining in their company and simply ignored the stranger. Tiana, however, could not take her eyes off of him. The stranger's appearance wasn't unusual or out of place. His face revealed nothing as to his way of thought. But there was something about him that scared her. Whatever it was that set her on edge, it told her he was a dangerous individual.

While she was trying to rid her serving tray of drinks, she could not help but keep an eye focused on the newcomer. Try as she might, she was helpless to resist stealing quick glances at him. Fortunately, Tiana returned her thought back to what she was doing and avoided dousing a customer in ale. It was when she read the words, 'This should prove amusing,' on his lips, she decided that now might be a good time to take a brief break.

3

"This should prove amusing," Lucian spoke softly to himself.

The once-dead warrior reflected on years past and sensed that times had not changed much. Especially when it came to town drunks. The patrons inside here were no different from those of his era: stupid, obnoxious and foolhardy. True, the latter of the three had yet to be proven, but Lucian was willing to predict it's surfacing.

To his eyes, the intoxicated men disgusted him. They had no motivation to conquer or control their ambitions and dreams. These men were cowardly and had to rely on alcohol to quench them of their demons. They had no self control over their emotions. They cared not for what the next day would bring as long as they could drown their pains tonight. These were just the pawns he needed to obtain.

Breaking away from his thoughts, Lucian slowly walked toward to the room's center. Along the way he snatched a frosty mug from a rather nervous barmaid and claimed it for his own. The startled girl managed to keep her composure and carry on with her job, he both noted and admired.

"I am looking for an item stolen from me." Lucian was not one to waste words or time. "A sword, to be exact. The blade shimmers like moonlight, and a woman fashioned is on its hilt, cast in gold."

The room occupants silenced themselves.

"I think I might have your sword, little boy," Rhon spoke up amidst his group of chuckling friends. "In fact, I think I've had it for a while."

"Oh, really," Lucian directed his attention to the obvious liar. A crooked smirk formed on his face. "Do tell."

Standing up with the help of the table and a friend at either side of him, Rhon proceeded to untie the rope-belt around his trousers and pull them down to his knees. "It might not shine in the moonlight, but it almost always has a woman fashioned to it," he roared.

Lucian twitched his right fingers and widened his smile.

The room was in hysterics over Rhon's rude gesture until he exposed what everybody thought was going to be his penis. But, instead of the expected male organ, a black serpent stretched out. Screams of horror and confusion filled the room. None more bloodcurdling that Rhon's, though.

Falling backwards over his own chair, he landed on his back and instantly sobered up. His friends could only watch in dumb confusion as they tried in vain to understand what was happening. "HELP ME!!!" he screamed to the stunned crowd who chose to simply stare and watch the man grasp a hold of the serpent with both hands. Struggling to keep a grip, Rhon managed to slide his hand up the creature's slick body and prevent the head from striking. While doing this, he managed to free one hand, retrieve a small dagger he kept on him and sever the thing in half.

It was when the illusion had faded and Rhon realized he

had just mutilated himself that he wailed out screams that truly chilled their blood.

Ignoring the outburst in the corner, Lucian granted his audience with a second chance. "I am looking for a sword that was stolen from me. Has anybody seen it?"

4

M'Kayla fathomed that she was going to spend another restless night after her nightly meeting with Kort. It was to be the same as every other night. Had she not been out of contact with the Circle for so long, she would have picked up on Lucian's entrance much earlier than she did. However, that point was irrelevant now.

The old woman had just sat herself down by the fireplace and finished tucking a thin blanket around her weakened knees, when he entered. She refused to grant him a brief moment of her attention. After all, the only people who ever entered these walls, especially this time of night, were those who yearned for the alcohol to consume them into a childlike glee. Their constant presence unnerved her when she first took up residence here, now she understood they needed to be here as much as she did.

It had taken M'Kayla months to figure out the inn's role. It was not merely a shelter for those who wished to rest in their travels. It was more of a safe haven for those whom life had no further used of. Desperate souls scattered throughout the rooms hoping to find an answer to better their life. Most, unfortunately, only captured a drunken stupor. But, as stated earlier, M'Kayla knew she belonged here. She had long since tired herself out from running away from her past. Her soul was no different from any of the others who occupied this inn at any given time. Until now.

The tiny grayed hair on her neck stiffened after the newest stranger gave a description of his sword. It was then that she realized just who had entered through the doors. This realization weakened her control and she felt helpless as she gave Lucian her full attention. She only prayed that he would fail to notice her.

5

In his right hand, Lucian kept a firm grasp on the mug of ale as he clutched it from the top with his index finger stirring the drink's frosty surface. He waited for the group to calm down and soak in his repeated question. He did not have to wait long.

A chair swung out at Lucian. The sound it made as it parted the air was all that was needed for him to prepare for it's coming.

The chair's wielder was Thak Clayborne. Mild in nature, he generally stood by and watched the world fold out before him. He usually bore no ill will toward anyone, for anything. Tonight, unfortunately, the ale was speaking for him. It was midday when he had lifted his first intoxicating mug to his lips and he had consumed enough during the past several hours to let it do a lot of talking.

The chair had only inches to go when Lucian moved out of harm's way. A simple sidestep would have been sufficient. Move forward, let the object whiz past his head and the threat would have been over. Lucian had another idea, though.

The rest of the patrons were not as bewildered as Thak, when his young target 'blinked' away. The boy was standing there one second, then four feet away the next second. But, Lucian was not the only one who moved. Thak did, too.

For a brief moment in time, Thak existed in two places at once. One right in front of the second one. The displaced Thak only served one purpose: to hit himself with his own chair. Which he did. Upon impact, the hard, wooden legs of the weapon cracked as it split open the back of the confused man's head. The former image of the drunk had dissipated before the transported, and injured, one hit the floor.

Lucian stood calmly, while he casually looked down at his fallen victim and kept stirring his ale with his finger.

It was then that the stupidity of mankind sparked to life. The merry feeling of fellowship the proprietors of *Kym's Keep* once possessed, had erupted into a fierce, out-and-out brawl. It did not matter to them the samples of power they had laid eyes upon. It did not even dawn on them that they stood no chance of defeating a person of this caliber. After all, they were drunk. They were stupid and they were men. Being male, they had no choice but to fight the doomed battle, for three reasons: 1.) they were on their home soil, 2.) they had an inner pride to defend their honor and 3.) they could not make themselves look weak in front of the women present. True, the latter one was the one that drove them the hardest. They did not want to be branded cowards by them, if they survived.

Needless to say, Lucian was somewhat disappointed with the men's performance. He had hoped after all these years that man would have been taught a better style of fighting. Alas, he saw it was the same as it was in his own time: they fought with their fists instead of their heads. There were at least fifty or more men, Lucia gathered and none could formulate any sort of reasonable method of attack. They were simply engaged in a large free-for-all.

A large man, built as he had been borne amongst ogres, whimpered while he cradled his shattered fist with his good arm. He had decided to throw a basic fist aimed at the boy's face and had actually connected. Sort of. The fist was crushed by a protective shield that surrounded Lucian. The barrier was only a hair's width away from his body and it refused to give any leeway.

Another fool had cast a spell derived from an old medallion passed on throughout the generations of his family. With the heirloom's metal backing resting on the man's outstretched palm, he set out a stream of acid in Lucian's direction. This, too, was easily countered as it was divided into two deadly lines by a small breath of air that Lucian blew on it as it neared him. The acid quickly washed over several combatants who were on either side of the ancient evil.

The battle continued on in this nature for the next several minutes. Each man had taken a shot at the arrogant youth and none succeeded in their attempt. Some simply were defeated with nothing more than a dislocated joint or a minor gash. Others suffered broken limbs, shattered noses, punctured eyes, but a few were dealt with fatalities. Among the list of those who were lost were: Rhon, who bled to death from his self-inflicted wound, and the bard Lyn, who fell victim to the earlier acid bath. He had the misfortune of ingesting a large portion of the deadly liquid, when his jaw dropped in horror as it had approached.

Nearing the end of the brawl, Lucian stood calmly in the center of the room, never once flinching from an attack. His emotions remained frozen while his inner disgust grew toward these weaklings. Though their attacks constantly failed, they were still too ignorant, in his eyes, to surrender to his higher power. Part of him did admire their courage to continue the fight, but the rest of him saw this act for what it was: the stupidity of man.

The room was struck silent within a heartbeat of time. For those who were not left dead or unconscious, they ceased all actions once they witnessed what seemed like the impossible. While the rest of the people were fighting, throwing anything within reach or helping a friend recover from a failed attack, M'Kayla marched a straight line to Lucian and briskly slapped him across the face. Though this form of attack should not have produced the hushed reaction, the fact that she actually came and inflicted the night's first blow to the untouchable one, did.

The second her hand left his face, M'Kayla readied herself for Lucian's retaliation. The man before her made the depth of her soul quake with fear. But, the suspicion that if she would not have cowardly hidden her identity earlier, none of these lives would have been lost, forced her to stand her ground, despite her maddening urge to flee.

Lucian reeled back, as startled as everyone else was. Fury began to boil up inside of him. The mighty Lucian had been struck by an ancient relic of a woman. *How dare she?! Does she not realize whom she stands before?* Then, his growing anger slowly diminished. The look in her eyes told him that she was terrified . . . yet determined. She could not have been blinded to his display of power. Surly, she was aware that he could extinguish her life with nothing more than a mere snap of his fingers. But, she had the nerve . . . to hit . . . him?

She knows me!

He scanned her face, looking for anything to tell him just who she was. He could not pick up anything from her eyes or facial expressions except for fear.

Then he leaned closer to her. Not physically, but mystically. His stare bore right through her with the intent of penetrating the secrets of her soul only to be violently denied. His brain screamed fiercely from the mental defenses set up in M'kayla's mind.

The attack lasted for all of one second. The aftershock, however, took a bit longer to wear off. Forced to take a step back, Lucian was barely able to recapture his balance. His mind was engulfed in anguish. Then it was over like it never happened in the first place.

"You wench!" he bellowed. Tiny droplets of spit spattered onto the old woman's face.

Lucian's right hand sprung out like a coiled snake and latched onto her neck. Using fury to feed his strength, he picked her up, carried her halfway across the room and slammed her back up against the nearest wall. "Who are you?!"

Even if she wanted to, M'kayla was in no position to answer the mad man. Her hands were clutched onto her attacker's arm and trying to pull herself up to avoid choking. She wasn't succeeding.

Lucian left her hanging a bit longer, so she could get a better sense of his power. His hand tightened as he debated on whether he wanted to wait for some answers from her or to simply crush her throat. His warrior training had reminded him that, 'To destroy the enemy, you must, first, know the enemy.' He forced himself to loosen his grip enough for her to capture her breath and lowered her back to her feet.

M'Kayla still held onto his arm while she replenished her lungs. The temporary loss of oxygen had begun to make her lightheaded and she had to shake way the effects.

Lucian sensed that control of the situation was reverting back to him, again. He still had the urge to strangle the old woman, but that emotion had already dissipated enough to avoid acting upon it.

While he had the mysterious woman held in place, he took a moment to listen to and check up on the rest of the room's occupants. It seemed as if they had learned their lesson. Those who were left alive merely tended to their own wounds now, or simply watched on. Fearful of their lives, they held themselves in place and prayed to be overlooked by the demon of death. If they didn't move, or draw attention to themselves, they might be spared and survive to tell this tale.

As M'Kayla stood gasping for air, Lucian started to take more notice of her. With her mouth wide open, he saw the source of the problem.

"I see someone has dealt with you before, wench," he said in reference to her blackened stump of a tongue. "I shall admit that you are full of surprises. Your mere presence is a sheer mystery to me, old woman. You know who I am, don't you?"

The look on her face betrayed her desire to hide the truth.

"Your talents to withstand my thoughts are impressive. Only those who harness a strong enough will . . . " Lucian paused to focus on a sudden thought. ". . . or are *taught* to protect their thoughts can withstand a probe."

Her face betrayed her, again.

"The Circle taught you well."

"The Circle?" someone dared to whisper aloud.

"But, the Circle of Elders is a rumored myth," another added to the hushed round of confusion. "Are they not?"

While the injured patrons dealt with the newfound knowledge of sharing a room with a member of the fabled Circle and found hope growing in their hearts, some were more confused than others.

Random thoughts then began to spring up throughout the room:

If she is of the Circle, surely she can save us.

She was here, amongst us, all this time?! Perhaps, then, there are others who can come to our aid.

Why is one of the Circle frightened of a boy?

What is the Circle of Elders, anyway?

Hidden in the kitchen area, Kort fought with Tiana. The lad was worried for his friend's safety and she was concerned for the child's welfare.

"Let me go!" he cried.

"Kort, listen to me. Wren can take care of himself. You need to stay here, where it is safe," she said.

"But, he's going to kill M'kayla!" the boy pleaded in hopes of being freed from the waitress's protective arms.

"And if she dies, then you will follow just as quickly," she warned.

Pausing for a moment, Tiana's ears caught up with her mind. A question then was forced through her lips, "Who's M'kayla?"

Kort looked at the edgy woman with a puzzled expression. It took him a moment to remember that he was the only person who knew the old woman by her birth name. Extending out a shaky finger, he pointed out the lady being threatened by the mad man, "The old woman, she's my friend."

A sigh of pity seeped out of Tiana

"He's hurting her, Tiana. I have to do something."

She knew he was right. *What could a child of twelve do, though, against someone that powerful?* She did not know.

While lost in thought, she was soon to get her answer. Kort had managed to slip through her slacked arms and was heading toward the center of the conflict.

Tiana had to force down a cry of warning to the boy, out

of fear her words would only draw the evil one's attention to both of them. Before, she was content enough to stay hidden behind the kitchen counter. Now, she had no choice but to leave the safety of her shelter behind. All because the boy wanted to protect a strange old woman.

6

Kort flew into the room and made no attempt to hide his presence. His screams of "Leave her alone!" would have made any attempt futile, anyway. Whether you want to call his actions noble or stupid, he kept his speedy course toward M'kayla and her tormentor.

A slight chuckle bellowed out from Lucian. *They even breed their offspring to be foolhardy.* With a raise from his left hand he decided to deal with this little menace swiftly, so he could get back to the business at had. A simple flick from his hand would have forced the kid backwards, slamming him into the serving wench who was following right behind. Unfortunately, the gesture failed to come about. He forgot about the dead fingers he still had trouble to adjusting to.

Needless to say, Kort was shocked to have reached his destination. Having done so, he was at a loss as to what to do next. With no better ideas to act on, he simply started to beat Lucian's back with his balled-up fists. "Let her go! She's done nothing to you . . . you big meany!"

"Go back to nursing off of your mother, brat," he warned and successfully swatted him away, causing a red welt to form across the lad's face.

Tiana, still chasing after Kort, leapt over and grabbed him. Her momentum carried them past Lucian and landed them underneath a table that miraculously was left standing in all the commotion. Once under the oak structure, the frightened waitress clutched ahold of the bruised boy and swore to herself that she would not let him go again.

Though Kort failed to bring about any of the real harm he had intended to inflict upon Lucian, he did manage to succeed in something. He had served as a distraction.

Now, being held in place, M'kayla was the object of pity for most of the inn's occupants. Thin strands of her grayed hair were matted across her forehead with the nervous sweat she was producing. The bags under her eyes became more apparent. Also, her thin frame, compared to Lucian's, convinced everybody of her helplessness.

Even though she projected the notion of weakness, she was far from defenseless.

Careful not to move too much, so not to revert his attention back to her yet, M'kayla moved her hands up to her mouth. Now that her feet were firmly grounded again, this was not much of a problem.

It felt like ages since she vowed to abandon her beliefs, but now realized she had no choice on whether to break them or not. So, when Kort provided her the moment she needed to act out against her aggressor - she took it.

The memories of her past teachings flowed back into her mind like a dam's gate releasing the vast amounts of water it held back. Her thoughts took her back to her first steps away from the Circle of Elders' protective realm. She relived each and every encounter since that point, both good and bad. How she wished she could stop the uncontrollable re-enactments. She had hoped to forever bury the dreadful memories of her bouts with Alista.

Damn that Alista! How one person could strive to be the bane of another person's existence, sickened her. She left the Circle to quest for knowledge and never intended to create a nemesis out of Alista.

She wished she had been a little more prepared to encounter a foe, when she had felt it was time to leave. What evil had sent the woman toward her? Was it the association with the Circle? Did she embarrass the woman, somehow? Or, was it something completely simple and foreign to her? Whatever sparked the resentment, it stuck with her up until their last fatal encounter. It was at that fateful meeting when M'kayla swore her sacred vow and placed herself in isolation. Until now, she thought she had managed to hide from her past. How foolish she was to believe that. But now was not the time for such thoughts. They would have to wait for another day.

She prayed that her memories did not steal too much away from the precious time that she needed.

With no more thoughts pondering the past or future, the old woman did what she needed to do, in the present. Having clasped her hands over her mouth, she began to mentally call out to the gods, . . . and prayed that they would still listen to her.

'Great and mighty spirits above

grant your lost child's cry and plea

Please mend what once was lost

and cleanse my soul, I beg of thee

We ask you to send this evil away

this moment, this instant, this very day

Transport this demon from this ground he stands on

and with a single spoken word, let this present threat . . . "

*   *   *

Lucian, finished with the kid's interference, focused back on M'kayla. He knew, later, the mistake he had made. But, when he reached that conclusion, it just did not matter.

M'kayla held off the final word to her prayer until Lucian reestablished eye contact. She could have ended this several moments ago, but waited until she had gained some personal satisfaction. She wanted Lucian to curse her name, knowing that he was bested by a decrepit, old woman. She received her wish.

Her eyes locked onto Lucian and rewarded his venomous gaze with a cocky smirk she revealed when she removed the hands covering her mouth. She kept her hands by her head and showed him her palms as if to say, 'See. Nothing up my sleeves'. Then, her expressions turned cold and serious.

Lucian raised an eyebrow to display his sudden confusion.

"....BEGONE!" M'kayla, daughter of the Circle of Elders, blared with the gift of her reformed tongue.

Startled, amazed, puzzled or furious, it just did not matter what Lucian's reaction was. It just depended on who is telling the story. Most of the survivors from *Kym's Keep* would say that it was

172

fear that overwhelmed him at that moment. What mattered, though, was that he was gone.

As quickly as they could blink their eyes, the man they would never come to know as Lucian simply was not there anymore. M'kayla instantly felt the pressure released from her throat, slid her back down the wall and sat her drained, tired body on the ground.

"Oh, praised and blessed be! Your child thanks you for your aid," she whispered in a weak, raspy voice. The rush from all the excitement and drain from the magick had taken its toll on the elderly woman. Though she was far from dying, she did have an overwhelming urge to rest and right there against the wall was just fine with her.

It took the members of Karsonis a few minutes before they dared to move. Some had witnessed Lucian's sudden departure and were still afraid to leave their personal safe havens. That was why Kort took so long to rush over to M'kayla.

"He's gone," the boy kept trying to tell Tiana. But, of course, since she did not witness the event, she was hesitant on believing the lad. She was along the lines of thinking it was another one of his tricks to get over and save his friend. When she saw that some people were walking around in a drunken stupor, she started to hope that his words were true. Her grip then loosened enough for him to escape it again, and head toward the old woman. This time, she did not go chasing after him. She, instead, stood up and joined the others as they nervously looked around to see if the evil truly was gone.

"Did he hurt you, M'kayla?" was the first thing he asked when he reached her side.

It was difficult for her mouth to remember how to speak, after all of those years without the use of her tongue. Despite the slight slur her words carried, it was still good to be able to talk, again. "I'll be fine, dear," she assured him as she very slowly lifted up a hand and affectionately ruffled up the boy's hair.

"Did you kill him? Is that what you did? I knew he couldn't stand up to you," Kort rambled on.

"I didn't kill him," she corrected him. "I . . ." she stopped and looked skyward, " . . . *we* just sent him far away from here."

"Where?"

"I don't know," she admitted and then she gave the boy a brisk hug to hide her frightened tears just as Wren found Kort and gave a backbreaking hug of his own.

"Dad . . . " Kort tried to convey through gasps of breath. "You got . . . to stop . . . that. My back can't take . . . much more."

Still, Wren did not care. He was just happy to still have his son. So, he issued out another hug.

CHAPTER EIGHT

Gessa was unsure of how far she had traveled from the shrine. She was just as clueless as to the length of time that had passed. If not for the fact that the ground offered too much comfort for her to move her shattered body, she would have been able to obtain the answers to both of those questions. She could have looked over the patches of bushes to see the sun's position and determine the time. At the same instant, she would have been able to see the shrine, still visible, a couple hundred yards away.

Though her mind screamed for her to continue on, her body had won the battle of wills. She could not bring herself to move. Her last act of strength had been depleted after she rolled herself over to rest on her back.

The pain seemed almost distant, now. Her memory came to her in pieces. For now, the battered young woman was happy to feel her chest rise and fall as she took short, shallow breaths. She thought she heard birds nestled in the trees, but most of that was drowned out by the sound of her heart pumping and blood circulating. Ba-boom. Ba-boom. Ba-boom. The sound could have driven her to madness. That is, if she was still coherent enough to care.

2

Gessa was barely aware that she had blacked out. She

could only guess by the light of the moon that she had lost a couple hours of consciousness. Even still, she was too weak and exhausted to put much thought on the issue.

Moments later, she had succumbed into the black void of slumber. No dreams intruded upon her mind as she crept closer to death.

3

Gessa woke to the familiar scent of burning wood and what smelled like roasted meat. It was not the aroma alone that roused the woman, but what it could be associated with. Was the forest on fire? Was she?! If not, who was and where?

The answer she craved had to wait until her opened eyes adjusted to the bright morning sun. Instinctively, Gessa sat up and shielded her eyes with her forearm, then regretted the action, just as soon. Her ribs protested their sudden strain and forced her back to the ground, again.

"Just let me die, already," she surrendered to whoever.

"I would rather not, my child," a calm, fatherly voice said to her.

"Sarvon?" Gessa asked with a hint of disbelief. Was she dreaming? Or dead?

"A far cry from, Gessa," the voice told her. "Now, rest. You still need to heal some more."

A fuzzy image of a man appeared in Gessa's vision and was silhouetted by the sun's rays.

"Gunthar? Is that you?" she faintly asked and followed up with a nasty chain of coughs.

176

"Yes, it's me," the grinning librarian revealed. "Now, like I said, you still need to heal some more. So, just lie there and rest or you'll undo everything I've done to heal your wounds."

Gessa had a stronger belief that the advice came from her state of delirium than from the actual person. To think that he would have come out here, all this way to save her, was too unlikely.

Nevertheless, she listened to the kind words and soon drifted off into a rather peaceful sleep.

4

Gunthar returned to his seat by the warm campfire and continued to watch vigilantly over Gessa. The new morning sun had just begun to warm the crisp night air about an hour ago.

Shifting around to find a comfortable position against a small, uprooted tree, the middle-aged librarian/wizard wished for his youthful attributes to return. He recalled, as a young lad, being quite physical; climbing trees, building forts, evading bothersome brothers and sisters. The memories were pleasant and brought back a lot of warm, tender moments. It also had a way of reminding him that time had passed and his body had grown old. By far, he was not hindered by his age, the way some of the older wizards of the Circle were, but being confined to a chamber of books had a way of making the human body weak and lazy. That is, if you let that happen, as Gunthar had.

"I'm too old for this much excitement," he told himself.

After grumbling awhile longer about his sore back and

aching legs, Gunthar returned his attention back to the chunk of rabbit meat roasting over the campfire. By appearances, the food looked cooked enough. But, weary of his own judgment, he decided to wait and let it set in the fire some more.

How coincidental it had been, finding her there. Granted, she was not in the condition he had expected. He had prayed his thanks to the gods for discovering her in time. She would have surely died if he had had second thoughts about venturing out. Maybe it was fate that pushed him along. After all, she was the reason he took his temporary leave from his home.

Gunthar was not the quickest thinking man to dwell in the Circle's fortress. But, he was far from the slowest. He was a man who liked to think without the pressure of having to do so. He liked to think things through and keep his ears open. He was never quick to judge or second-guess a situation. He was more prone to wait for more information, so he would have a better understanding of what, or who, he was facing.

It had been a day since he had seen Gessa and her companions off. He had been in his usual surroundings, sorting through borrowed books and placing them back in their designated positions. That's when what he called the 'thought catalyst' kicked in.

Gunthar had been putting away a series of books when it happened. His thoughts had kept a constantly worried tone stemming toward Gessa and why the council had sent her out after Lucian. They had to know that she was no match for that monster. They must have had their reasons, but still, he could not help feeling concerned.

Anyway, while his mind was stuck on Gessa, he kept busy. It was when he began associating book topics with Lucian as he was putting them away, that things started to come together. None of the books he reshelved dealt directly with Lucian. The subjects ranged from past threats to the Circle, to Elven magick, to the way of the lands over the past couple of centuries, to name a few. There were plenty of books dealing directly with Lucian, some of which he had lent out to Gessa. The rest had not been touched in years. When Gunthar had finished stocking, he took a moment to reflect and focus.

To do his job correctly, he had to catalog each student's history of borrowed items. This was done to ensure that each pupil could not falter on the excuse of not obtaining the books. More importantly, it was a way for teachers to keep track of what subjects their students were actually studying up on in their free time.

Of course, this was not the only method the Circle used to keep tabs. A number of spells were cast to safeguard their knowledge, as well. For example, no book, scroll or parchment could be taken out of the library without Gunthar's seal of enchantment that would materialize the item back to the library should it be lost of stolen. Another spell was placed on the students, rather than the literature. All students had access to every book the Circle possessed, except for each Master's private collection. This particular spell worked in two ways. 1.) If a student was not ready to handle the responsibilities of a higher form of magick, the book simply would not open for them. 2.)

On the same note, if that student were to view the pages with purposeful intent, either by having someone else open the book, glancing over the shoulder of whoever was reading it or any other means, they suffered a temporary loss of sight which was followed by an appropriate punishment delivered by the Elders. Some had knowledge taken from their minds and were forced to relearn earlier lessons. Others faced stiffer sentences like having their minds erased of all desire to learning magick and were then banished. The Circle of Elders felt no sympathy toward those too eager or those who had abusive designs for their magick.

The other method Gunthar chose to use, of his own design, was one that only few were privileged to. To keep aware of the books that were not borrowed out, an enchantment was placed on the furnishings in the room. Once a book or scroll was placed upon a table, the table would read and record the student's name, what they were reading and what pages they spent the most time reading. It was a very complex spell to have been constructed. Gunthar was quite proud of his accomplishment, considering it was one of the first spells he constructed when he took over the job as librarian.

The extraction of the information took Gunthar some time to perform. It was not a simple matter of walking over to one table and getting the answers he wanted. No, each table held its own records. So he painstakingly went to each of the three hundred ninety-seven enchanted tables that filled the massive space the library offered.

Four hours and thirty-six minutes after he began, Gunthar

found the one table that offered him the answers he was searching for. At that point, the forty-seven-year-old Keeper of the Scrolls made a silent vow to link all of the enchanted tables into one interlocking system.

With his hands laid palms down upon a table located in an obscured corner, Gunthar closed his eyes and concentrated. Being a person committed to his work, he found himself shocked to discover that he was almost deceived in his own library.

The table allowed him to clearly see through its surface, as if he was looking through his own eyes at the books read by the person who chose to sit there in the past. It was when he saw the dust-covered volumes detailing every account and action committed by Lucian that he began to realize what he found.

Considering the numerous students and masters who spent time within the book-covered walls, it would be impossible to direct the tables to run through each person individually, so he mainly concentrated on anything that might be linked to the evil one. He never expected to find the actual chronicles of Lucian's life being read.

Since the books were never checked out, Gunthar had ignored their possible use. After all, they still had dust accumulated on them. It was then that he realized he had been duped. The dust was nothing more than a well-constructed camouflage.

The instant Thomas's face was revealed, Gunthar broke off his contact and sped off to address the Elders.

5

Gunthar couldn't remember the last time he stood outside of the Circles's mountain-based domain. The feeling was both disturbing and refreshing. It was good to explore the outside world, but he was worried that isolation would leave him too naive of the ways of society.

Trotting along on Elvira, a brown quarter horse borrowed from his good friend and peer, Master Wade, Gunthar was on his way to search for Gessa. He had to warn her of his discoveries and prayed he was wrong about Thomas. Could the child be a secret follower of Lucian or was his research just a simple focus of curiosity? That was what worried him. He had to find out, whatever the answer may be. He hated unanswered problems and he was determined to resolve this one.

It had been a tough journey that brought him to Lucian's shrine. Elvira, he sensed, had enough of traveling, too. Her slow trot was just one clue that led him to that belief. Whenever the mare reared her determined resistance of moving any further, Gunthar knew he had arrived. Taking the precaution of tightly securing Elvira's reigns to a massive oak's unearthed root, Gunthar worriedly made his way to the sanctuary.

It hardly took any time to determine the events that transpired within the immortal walls. All he had to do was look at the rotting corpse of Opal spread out upon the floor to see what happened. Terror stabbed at his heart as he raced throughout the building in hopes of finding the other children.

By counting the charred ribs of the only other body the room held, Gunthar was fairly certain he stood over top of

Thomas. The bone's length puzzled him, however. He would have guessed the boy's skeletal frame would have been a little bit smaller. *Maybe this was someone else*, he considered.

Normally, he would have spent longer to resolve the issue. The urge to find the other child, Gessa, forced him to place that problem in the back of his mind for later.

Between the death songs hummed by the swarming flies and his hurried, if somewhat sloppy, search tactics, he was running in circles in a desperate attempt to find something. He would have settled for anything that could lead him to Gessa's whereabouts. He had gone over the area twice and was about ready to make it a third time. Then, his unspoken prayers were fulfilled.

A twinkle of light caught hold of his attention, from across the room. Curious of its origin, Gunthar was soon to discover the light was a reflection off of the gold ring wrapped around Opal's right ring finger. The sunlight had peered through the open doorway to spread a small patch of light into the room.

He saw this as a sign from Sarvon.

It was not the ring that he took for a sign, but the position of the dead girl's arm. It looked to him like she was pointing toward the door's opening, as if to say, 'She's out there! Hurry! There's still time!'

In his hasty approach to finding his missing clue, the obvious had eluded him. Until now. Streaks of blood that he initially guessed as belonging to Opal, were caked to the floor and led toward the outside. He now understood what he was meant to find. The blood could not have been Opal's. It started, at least, a good foot from where the girl lay. It must, though he prayed it was not, be Gessa's. He moved with renewed determination and sprinted out the door into the sun's warm presence.

The dark tracks of blood staining the open field became suddenly clear to him. From his angle of view, he also saw the matted and torn patches of grass snaking its course out into the darkened woods.

The winds picked up and shifted its chilled breeze to push Gunthar along as he sprinted down to the track's end. That was where he found Gessa. Her crippled form and blood-soaked shreds of clothing cast the belief that he was too late.

"Great Sarvon! No! Please let there be time!" he cried as his knees crashed into the cold dirt beside the girl's fallen form.

A weakened moan formed from Gessa's lips and wrenched Gunthar's weeping head up from its slumped position. "Blessed be!" his raised head praised skyward, in thanks. Wasting no more time, the aged librarian went to work at mending the poor girl's broken body.

6

It's late and nightfall will be coming soon, Gunthar fathomed as he continued his vigil. After Gessa had recovered to the point where he felt it was safe enough to transport her, he moved her back into Lucian's enchanted field. He knew they would be safe in there from the forest's predators. Judging from his horse's reaction, he was fairly sure no animal wanted to even be close to the evil ground they occupied.

With a nice blazing fire to warm them throughout the night, the thin man removed himself from his resting spot to tend to Elvira. This was a ritual he had followed for the past few nights.

He had pity for his borrowed horse for not being able to be with them in the grassy plain. The horse simply refused to go. So she had to settle for another night of an oat bag and a short trip to a nearby stream to get her fill of water until the morning.

Upon his return to the makeshift campsite, Gunthar saw his patient had fully awaken. Though her wounds ached her enough to keep her resting on the ground, the rest of the night was spent with the two of them sharing the events that brought had them together.

CHAPTER NINE

"Hurry, I sense his approach!" I heard the Elder Kane urge.

I remember that we were within my husband's personal study when he spoke those words to me. I tried to heed his warning, but I knew it was too late. With one single door available to enter and exit, I was certain to be found. Kane also knew this to be true. My husband's bellowing cries of my name and the loud slaps of his angered footsteps told me that we only had seconds left.

Using only the time it took me to turn my head to witness him, the mysterious man of magick shifted his form into that of a small, black, house cat. It was the first time I had ever seen the workings of true magick performed before my eyes.

Kane's transformation had shaved, ever so closely, to the workings of time because, the instant he finished, Lucian came crashing through the doorway.

"Sasha! What in Taukin's blazing pit are you doing in my private chambers?!"

I was quick to respond to his heated temper. I lowered my head, so not to have him read the lie on my face, "I was looking for you, my love."

"You have found me, woman." The coldness of his tone still chills my soul. "What do you want with me?"

"Can't a woman seek out her husband, merely for his

company?" I replied with another falsehood. "I got lonely and thought to look for you here. When I saw the room was absent of your presence, I decided to wait. You spend most of your time in here, so I knew your return would not be long in coming."

I hated to lower myself to such a pretentious level when I was around him. Alas, circumstances had forced me to stay in that role, if only for appearance's sake. I have come to accept the man I once loved was dead and only an evil shell of his being walked in his place. I have seen his wrath extend out toward those who slightly questioned or foolishly challenged his words.

"Be on your way. I don't have time for such trivial nonsense. I have work I must attend to."

I could tell he saw through my deceit, just by the way his eyes kept narrowing.

As I turned to leave, I felt a softness rubbing itself up against my bare ankles. With the fear building in me of suffering my husband's anger, again, I had completely forgotten about Kane.

Having scooped him up in my arms, I left that godforsaken room and moved down the cold, empty hallway. All the way to my bedroom chambers Kane kept his feline form. I think he rather enjoyed it when I was scratching behind his ear and rubbing his belly.

All the way to my chambers, where I felt we could continue our conversation in private, I kept reflecting on the artifacts Kane had shown me. I was aware of my husband's darkened change, but it was then that I knew just how evil he had become.

When we went into the room, we found that we were not

alone as predicted. Allena was waiting on me.

"Thank the gods that you are here," she praised the moment she laid eyes upon me.

"What troubles you, my friend?"

"I had to find you and send a warning of Lucian. His temper is more heated than usual. He was screaming out for you and I feared for your safety."

I placed Kane down on the soft, comfortable pillows and gave my lady-in-waiting a long, heartfelt hug we both needed.

"I have already dealt with him. His anger has diminished . . . for now. So, calm yourself, woman. I am safe."

She smiled back, pleased to see me in one piece.

"Allena? Might I request a cup of Kaillyn's spiced tea?" I asked her so I could have a few more minutes alone with the wizard.

To be honest, I needed the tea just as much, too. I have no idea what the old cook put into her herbal brew, but one sip always managed to soothe my troubled mind. She was the best damn cook we ever had.

"It would be my pleasure, M'lady," she answered with a slight curtsy.

"Get yourself one, too," I called out to her as she passed through the doorway.

I had watched until Allena rounded the corner and checked to be sure no others would be coming. "It's safe," I informed my guest as I turned back around.

Somewhere between my conversation with Allena and me

watching her leave, Kane had reverted back into the elder, silver-haired man he was. His crimson robe was back as well. I had hoped when he initially transformed that this would be the case. I did not relish seeing the man's aged and wrinkled body. The mere thought brought a swift wave of nausea, as I was forced to envision the picture; fortunately I managed to quickly overcome it.

"I have made certain of that," he replied. I had no idea what he meant by that statement. I think he wove a magickal spell. Without witnessing it though, I was forced to remain in the dark about his intent. "Did you see the truth, young one?"

"I never suspected what all that room held." I saw volumes upon volumes of journals, magickal text and miscellaneous others I was warned not to open or touch. It would be my guess that if the room had doubled in size, it would still appear cramped for space.

"No. Not the objects. They are mere tools. Nothing more," he reiterated with a gruff huff. "I refer to his nature."

I did not hesitate to give my answer. "Yes, I saw it, too. I wish I had not, though."

"It needed to be done," he simply stated.

"Why? What does this have to do with me? If he is as powerful as you say, how am I to aid you? He would surely kill me if he found out that we were even having this conversation."

Kane lowered his head and then looked upon me with nearly-defeated eyes. "I will repeat myself, for your benefit. I understand that this is very emotional and, likewise, unbelievable. Please listen carefully and bear with me. We do not have much

190

time before your servant returns."

"My friend," I corrected.

"Of course, 'your friend.' My apologies," he humbly admitted. "As I said before, my name is Kane. I come to you from a secret society known as the Circle of Elders. We are a people of magick who have sworn a solemn vow to protect and safeguard our world from the misuse and threat of the magick."

"I caught that much," I informed him.

"Anyway," he continued. "We have been observing the corruption of your husband's soul for some time. At first, we identified his behavior as simple greed. Being a king in power, we accepted this as nothing more than a typical human characteristic. When he began displaying his knack for complex magick, we came to realize the misjudgment we perpetrated.

"We had dispatched a small number of our order to handle Lucian. We had underestimated him, again, and lost seven of our strongest students," he explained.

"I heard nothing of this attack," I inserted.

"You weren't meant to. We had to maintain our status to the rest of the population, that of a myth. If we were to be identified as being real, we would suffer from evil's countless assaults and eventually fail in our mission."

Kane paused to recollect his thoughts after I interrupted. "By the time we got words of our group's defeat, Lucian was too powerful to attempt another confrontation. Besides, his expertise in military strategies would have allowed him to see us coming. So, we decided to pursue a different design of attack: we waited and watched.

"Whenever Lucian was in battle, we studied his fighting techniques. We sent spies out to witness his spell castings. The Circle had become dedicated to ending the threat of this one man.

"A prophetic dream came to one of the Elders and pointed us to you. You were then looked upon and studied, as well. It was noticed, after careful consideration, that you might be our only means of defense.

"Let's take, for example, our recent run-in with Lucian. By all rights, if you were any other person standing in his room, you would be dead. But, you're not. Why? Because, there is still a part of him that continues to love you. He saw past your lie and accepted it. Why? Because, you are a woman. You are weak and helpless in his mind. You are sworn to stand by his side and serve him. You are no threat."

"It sounds like you are wanting me to break that vow and betray him," I could not believe I was being asked this.

"That is what I am saying. Before you respond, again, let me ask you a question." Kane straightened himself up and forced me to see the seriousness in his words. "Which do you feel strongest about: the oath you made to your husband, your duty to protect the people of your kingdom, or the vow you made to never be weak or humble before a man's eyes, again?"

"You heard that?!" I blurted out. Those words were confined only to my thoughts. How can they know such things, I wondered.

"As I said, we are a people of magick," the old man grinned.

"More like intruders of one's privacy."

*"If it must be done to protect the innocents and the world around us, we won't hesitate to do so. You know as well as I do, Lucian is growing in power and there will reach a point where he **will** obtain a level power that will render us helpless before him. We must act soon, your highness."*

That was the first time he addressed me as royalty. I believe he was trying to convince me of my duty to protect the people of Jenna. He was playing dirty and had forced guilt upon me.

"Your servant, I mean, your friend is returning. I will remain here to await your answer."

Again, I witnessed his feline metamorphosis. No gestures or words were spoken by him to initiate the process. I saw his pupils enlarge and stretch into pointed ovals while his face contorted. His nose sunk back into his face as threads of whiskers sprouted around it. The color of his crimson robe darkened to black and was absorbed into his body while hair as black as a raven's feather grew all over his body into a full, shiny coat when his mass shrank to that of a cat's proper size.

When he was finished, Allena knocked and walked in with the requested tea. As we got to talking about anything that came to mind, like we usually did, Kane remained curled up on my lap, patiently waiting for my decision.

*   *   *

"Nix, are you even listening?" Twyla leaned closer to the seated man, prepared to deliver a swift welt across his face with her the flat of her palm.

His outstretched arms pushed a creeping yawn out of him. "What?! Huh . . . ?"

WHACK!!!

The force of the blow propelled the drowsy warrior to spin off of his chair and onto the hard, stone floor.

"What was that for?" Nix demanded as he rubbed the side of his face.

"Listen up! This is important. I didn't bring the two of you here for you to fall asleep." *I should have left them to wander out in the woods*, she thought to herself

Kelvin, the elven historian, could do nothing but stare at the two adults. It was a small wonder, he decided, that they have survived all these years without killing each other. *To think, our future rests in their hands. We might just very well be doomed*, he feared.

"Don't worry," Gavin said to the historian as he gnarled away on a stick of dried beef. "They do this all the time."

"Stay out of this, Gavin!" Twyla warned.

"See what I mean," Gavin pointed out.

With the sheathed hilt clutched in hand, Nix returned to his chair. With a watchful eye cast upon Twyla, he stole a moment to flash a quick nod signifying Kelvin to continue.

"As I was about to say," the elven recorder sighed. "The sword was the key to Lucian's reign. With it, he managed to eliminate two of his greatest weaknesses. So, it must not fall back into his possession."

"You mentioned, before, of a third," Twyla reminded.

"Indeed, I did. Alas, that one I am forbidden to address. As a historian, there are still some rules that I, too, need to follow. The answer, I assure you, will be revealed in time."

"Little help that does," mumbled Nix.

"Precisely, young man. Were I to hand over everything I know, you could defeat Lucian quite easily. However, you would learn nothing."

"Spare me the lessons in life," Nix gruffed. Rising up, he readjusted his light armor padding and motioned his group toward the door. "Come on, we wasted enough time here."

"Damnit, Nix, Jenna can wait! We need to find out as much as we can about this Lucian, first," Twyla argued.

"No, Twylanna, the warrior is right. You do need to reach the city."

"What do you know about the city of Jenna?" Nix demanded with renewed interest. Forgetting about the door, he went back to reclaim his chair and rejoin the conversation.

"Oh, I have your attention, now? Dear me, the honor, it overwhelms me," Kelvin mocked with sincerity.

"Spare me the act. Tell me what you know of Jenna."

"That's the problem with you humans," he voiced in disgust. "You only hear what you want to acknowledge. In doing so, you miss out on the rest of the picture, which is usually the important parts, because it's all so boring to you. Wake up and pay attention before the solution bypasses your wandering mind."

"Yeah, yeah, now . . . about Jenna?"

195

"You're smart, you will find out on your own . . . with any luck." With that, Kelvin rose from his chair and brushed away the wrinkles from his clothes. "I have given the three of you all the information that this moment calls for. I am forbidden to venture further in your quest for information. All I can say now, is you are heading down the proper path toward your destiny. But, be warned of beckoning side roads and be prepared to accept the consequences of what must be done."

"Could you be any more cryptic?" Nix asked.

"Yes, I can. But, then you would have to think harder for your answer." Addressing Twyla with a slight bow, Kelvin concluded the conversation. "I am afraid you must see yourselves off, now. You have a long road ahead of you. Be careful, Twylanna. May the gods see to your safe return." With a gentle hand resting on her shoulder, he escorted the trio out of his homestead. Uttering a soft prayer the instant the door closed, he asked the gods to extend Twylanna the patience to deal with the human warrior, as well.

2

If time could be slowed down to observe the millionths of a fractioned second that had passed while being transported, Lucian's brain would have fried from the overload of infinite beauty and knowledge. He would have witnessed the miracle of every child borne throughout history and felt the death of each one as darkness fell upon them. He would have seen the creation of all and have been a perceiver to the destruction of creation. He would know where his destiny was committed to take him and by what means his life would cease. He would see all, feel all, and know all. Fortunately, that die would not be cast.

The room in the inn.

The old woman he held by the throat.

That annoying brat who caused him to be distracted.

All were gone.

In their place, startled woodland creatures and ancient trees loomed overhead in a defiant attempt to shield the ground from the sun's heated gaze. The stench of blood and alcohol were substituted with the sweet scents of nature. All of that gone, and replaced in less time than it takes to bat an eye. The old woman had forced him away and relocated him in some unfamiliar forest setting. The mere thought of being rid of so easily sent his mind into rage. A novice would have seen that attack coming. His arrogant, overconfident ego blinded him and left him vulnerable. He would seek out his frustration on the old woman later. For now, the only thing Lucian focused on was nausea.

He was no stranger to travel by teleportation, as he proved back at the inn. Utilizing that kind of skill, one tends to grow accustomed to shifting from place to place, . . . if you are prepared. This time, Lucian was not. The flash of the disorienting environment wrenched pain throughout his body. Forced to fall to his knees, he was helpless to do anything but regurgitate his empty stomach. Collapsing from the expected wave of fatigue, Lucian curled on his side and simply laid on the grassy ground.

The minutes that passed crept by slowly. During that time, he tried to calm his jolted body and rethink his strategy. He had come to the conclusion that he was still too weak to continue the way he had been. The boy, Thomas, did not have the strength to ascend him to the level of power he required. The villagers added some to him, but it was still not sufficient. He needed more. He needed to find the thief who stole his sword. HIS SWORD!!!

Lucian's head snapped up. His face contorted into a puzzled expression. Looking around, his gaze surveyed the landscape. His sword . . . he felt it! It was close. Much closer than he sensed it in Karsonis. Then the reality of it all hit him. *The fool sent me straight toward it. My connection must have twisted her spell and practically delivered it into my hands!!!* The irony quenched his weakened state and renewed his spirits. Removing himself from the ground, he felt rejuvenated. The rage dwelling in him earlier was replaced with a fit of laughter. *Fools. The whole lot of them.*

3

The soft clapping of footsteps echoed down the darkened corridor. A cloaked figure, further masked by the dim lighting, quickened his pace as he tried to soften the impact of his footing. The task was not an easy one. The walls supporting the underground passage have long since weakened from stress and exposure. As a result, water from a nearby reserve allowed the walls to perspire and dampen the floors with small, muddy puddles.

Reaching his destination, the concealed man slipped out of the corridor and into a side room. A quick survey of the room revealed that he was the last of his companions to arrive and closed the heavy, wooden door behind him.

Young hands poked out of the elongated sleeves of the robe, once the door was locked. Then he moved them upwards to pull back the hood covering an equally young face. He glanced around to show the other occupants of the room his identity to ease their minds about being discovered.

Sensing he was about ready to speak, a robed woman hurried up to him and silenced his words with a finger to his lips. Pulling back her finger, she used it to signal him to wait a moment. Understanding the intent, he gave a simple head nod.

Watching the woman step back from him, he saw her hands glow and she waved them in all directions around herself. The woman, oddly enough, still disturbed him after all the time they worked together. It wasn't the fact that age was starting to show itself on her through the slight wrinkles and red, but greying, hairs. No, it was something else entirely. He related it to the feeling of being befriended, but still needing to check to see if his purse was there. Needless of how he felt about her personally, he respected her position as a Master.

After the female Master's hands stopped waving and the glowing faded away, the confining walls and ceiling glistened with a faint twinkle, including the door. "It is safe, now. The rest of the Elders cannot hear us," she informed him.

"I bring news of Lucian," the young man informed everybody.

"Does he walk amongst us, once more?" a male Elder demanded.

"Indeed, he does!" he grinned with pride.

"Blessed be!" the small group praised in hushed unison.

"Was Thomas able to carry out his mission and revive him?" another Elder questioned.

199

"I would assume so, but there are some issues that raise doubt to that." He went on to explain the ransacked shrine that he suspected was caused by looters. He mentioned the corpses littering the grounds and the burnt remains of a former pyre. "All of the students sent off have been eliminated, though"

"Their sacrifice was a necessary one. We needed someone that Lucian could feed off of, in his weakened state. Fortunately, that old fool, Kane, provided us with the pawns to use," the female Master addressed. "So, where is Lucian, now?"

"I do not know. I lost his trail in the town of Karsonis. He was there searching for the sword."

"The sword? You mean he's separated from it?"

"It would appear so. Apparently, the looters I mentioned earlier must be the ones responsible."

"Then, they must be hunted down and the sword retrieved!" an Elder demanded.

"But, we may have another problem. There's a new player that has been added, an old woman by the name of M'kayla"

"M'kayla? She's still alive!" the female Master exclaimed!

"I cannot answer that for certain. I arrived at a local tavern moments after they had an encounter with Lucian. A young boy, I overheard, called her by that name and spoke of the Circle. By the witnesses' accounts, she conjured up a magick spell and destroyed him. The description they gave leads me to believe she used a form of teleportation, instead. That's when I portaled back here."

"It would appear you have some matters you need to attend to, Alista," an Elder stated with a disappointing tone.

"I will take care of that wench, personally!"

"That's what you were suppose to do the last time, if I recall."

Snapping a cold, hard look at her superior, "I'll take care of it!"

"See that you do."

An Elder who had remained in the background, until now, briskly stepped into the center of the room. With a swift motion, he brought down the tip of his walking staff to strike the hard ground below. An abrupt burst of heated air erupted throughout the room, silencing everyone. "Enough!" Now that he had their attention, he said, "I will not have us feuding amongst ourselves. We have not waited all these years to see Lucian's return crumbled by happenstance circumstances and pointless bickering! We have been presented with our obstacles. Now, we must attend to them. Alista, go forth and investigate M'kayla's return. If it is her, I want to know if she's a threat or an act of coincidence."

"And if I feel that she is a threat?" Alista asked.

"You may dispense of her as you see fit. However, I want to know what she knows, first."

"I will do what I can," she added with a broad grin.

"Keep in mind, if she dies prematurely by your hands, you will die slowly by mine," the Elder stated matter-of-factly.

"Of course."

"As for this band of looters," the Elder continued, "We need to find them and reclaim the sword. This task I shall entrust to you, Derek. Hunt them down and kill them all."

Stepping forth from his place in the room, Derek positioned himself in front of the Elder. Dressed in a motley assortment of leathered armor and animal pelts, he was a killer of men with a hidden arsenal of weapons at his ready. Daggers were his weapon of choice. Twenty of them were strategically placed on his person. Still, that did not restrict him from sheathing a broad sword onto his back and a slingshot in a side purse. "And my fee?" he inquired through his scarred lips.

"Tripled, if you return the sword to us. Nothing, if you fail."

"Consider them dead already," Derek declared.

...To Be Continued!

ABOUT THE AUTHOR

Lowell Ellington lives in Canton, Ohio with his wife, Shelly, and son, Jacen. *The Sword's End: Book One* is his first published novel. He is currently working on *Book Two* and co-authoring a fantasy/satire novel with his longtime friend, Kevin Duffield. In addition to writing, he runs a novelty T-shirt shop on-line with Mr. Duffield. (www.gerbilsatemyunderwear.com)